DRIVING MISS DARCY

Copyright © 2019 by Sodasac Press

All rights reserved.

No part of this book may be reproduced in any form or by any electronic or mechanical means, including information storage and retrieval systems, without written permission from the author, except for the use of brief quotations in a book review.

Publisher: Sodasac Press

Cover design: Once Upon a Cover

Custom Artwork: Megan Shaffer

Editing: SJS Editorial Services

Formatting: Christina Butrum

1

GEORGIA

As I stepped out of the cab and skipped into La Guardia Airport a smile spread over my features at the prospect of five and a half blissful hours of in-flight entertainment eating a microwaved meal on a tiny tray. My friends at Juilliard thought I was crazy.

My dorm mate would say, "Georgia, you better bring a butt pillow." and "Make sure you chew gum to pop your ears."

She didn't care for planes.

But I really did love the solitude of sitting in a bucket seat, virtually undisturbed at thirty-eight thousand feet in the sky. I loved the prospect of traveling somewhere—even somewhere familiar—with the distinction of having woken up in a place thousands of miles away. When I traveled, I was someone who did things.

I could get into any kind of travel, really. If my movie star brother wasn't so annoyingly protective, I'd be all over the world satisfying my wanderlust with jaunts across Europe on romantic trains, or hiking to the tippy top of Machu Picchu. But today's trip was a trip home for Christmas. To a house my mother lovingly named Pemberley—because who doesn't name houses?

Granted, the house was the size of a shopping mall, so maybe that was her saucy sense of humor shining through.

My flight from cold, sludgy New York City to bright, breezy Los Angeles (with a connection in Chicago) would get me home just in time to wrap my Amazon orders and put them under the tree but also to attend my brother Will's wedding. He'd been with his girlfriend Beth almost a year.

The idea of a Christmas Day wedding would seem ludicrous to most people. But the holidays held something special for my brother and his bride, so who was I to warn them about all the potential stress? After all, what was the most major holiday on the planet to a high-profile Hollywood wedding? Santa Claus who? Will Darcy and Beth Bennet were getting married.

La Guardia was massive, but I wheeled my little carry-on bag through the terminal, spreading Yuletide cheer with each springy step as I made progress toward my gate. I envisioned magic Christmas dust sprinkling from my smiles and gleeful greetings as the TSA guards eyed me suspiciously. How dare I hum *Sleigh Bells* whilst passing though the security check? But I wasn't about to let those Scrooges cool my imaginary peppermint hot chocolate. No sir. I may have studied *Piano Concerto No 23* while school was in session, but *Jingle Bell Rock* was my jam.

Speaking of music, I fell asleep with my music app open on my cell phone and forgot to charge the battery. But since I had plenty of time before boarding, I decided to use one of the charging stations at the gate. I didn't account for the onslaught of holiday travelers, so all the charging ports were full. All except for one. Which was currently blocked by some guy's dog. He was ridiculously cute—the dog, not the guy. Okay, the guy, too. But neither the dog nor the man were the problem. It was the crowd of giggling girls surrounding them that really blocked my access to the charging port. All of them were young, barely out of high school by the looks of them, and they all wore spandex leggings a little too clingy around their backsides. I noticed this because those backsides were pointing directly at me as the girls bent over, fawning over the dog—and the man.

The dog, a jumpy little Jack Russell Terrier, was wagging his tail with unflagging abandon, joyfully licking their faces. The man, well he was enjoying the attention just as much. He probably only brought the dog along to get women's numbers.

"Excuse me." I said cheerily, holding out my phone. I pointed to the charging station. The girls all ignored me. "Um...excuse me?" I repeated a little louder this time. One of them turned around, standing up to her full height and stared at me for a whole three seconds before turning back to flirt with the guy. She was tall and slender and beautiful like all her friends and that look she gave me might as well have said *Back off, sister*.

"I just need to squeeze past you to charge my phone." I wanted to add *He's all yours*. I wasn't interested in the guy or the dog. My battery was at two percent; surely somebody would have mercy on me. I looked around me hoping to find an open port. Nope. Fancy businessmen in suits too important to give up their spots occupied half of the charging ports. The other half were occupied by teenagers—also not likely to unplug for little 'ol me. Not that height mattered. I wasn't as tall as that mean girl and her friends, but I more than made up for it in moxie. I got into Juilliard on my own merit, not because I had a famous brother. I was a strong woman, thank you very much. Small but mighty.

You got this, Georgia.

And so I rolled my shoulders back, lifted my chin, and tapped the girl on the shoulder.

She spun around so abruptly, the ripple effect of it disturbed her circle of friends and subsequently the adorable little dog. He barked—more of a *Hooray, a new friend!* sort of bark rather than a *Warning, Intruder alert* sort of bark. His owner looked up, deep dark eyes locking onto mine for one brief moment before the dog bounded off the charging port stool to greet me. The spandex brigade jumped back, Dog Man leaped up to reach for the leash, and cute little Jack Russell evaded him just quick enough to run circles around my feet—but not before his human hooked a finger on the leash's loop. As common knowledge of physics would dictate, my legs were wrapped in the leash and I came crashing down with all the spectacular force of gravity. As I landed with a glorious thud, my phone sprung from my hand and flew through the air like a determined little salmon swimming up a waterfall, narrowly missing the clutches of a hungry bear. It happened in slow motion—the crazy dog, falling on my bottom, my phone in flight. And yet it was like one of those nightmares where you feel like you're moving through molasses. The phone crashed to the floor with a definitive splat.

"Are you okay?" Dog Man said. He really did have beautiful eyes. I shook off that thought, remembering I was hurt and on the verge of tears, *not* ogling his handsomeness.

"What?"

"I'm so sorry about that." His nimble fingers were making quick work of the leash, untangling it from my ankles. The dog wasn't making it easy on him with all the tugging and bouncing. "Reeses, calm down."

So crazy dog had a cute name to match. Apparently *calm down* wasn't in Reeses' vocabulary. Presently, he was licking my hand.

"A little forward there, Reeses. We've only just met."

Dog Man chuckled and swooped up Reeses, offering me his other hand to help me up.

"I'll manage," I clipped, perhaps too forcefully. I probably shouldn't have snapped at him. He was trying to help me up after all. But the fall to the hard floor hurt my pride as well as my poor tooshie. I turned my eyes to my phone, shattered in a sad pile of bits of plastic and glass on the floor.

"Oh crud," I heard Dog Man say. "That sucks."

"That sucks?" I managed to say. It was then I noticed the makings of a suppressed laugh on his lips. "That...*sucks*?"

"I mean...I hope you have insurance."

I did, thanks to my brother, but that wasn't the point.

I forlornly scooped up the shrapnel surrounding my dead phone, mourning over it on my hands and knees. I promised Will I'd call him in Chicago between connecting flights and if I didn't he'd worry himself sick—just what a man needs a few days before his wedding.

"Here, let me help you," Dog Man said, no longer laughing at my expense at least.

"No thanks, dude."

"Listen, I—"

"Just please...go away." I was too embarrassed, and if I was being honest with myself, kinda attracted to Dog Man, which only made my face red.

So...Merry Christmas to me? The hap-happiest time of the year. Maybe.

2

GEORGIA

One would imagine airlines seated first-class passengers last—being closest to the front and all. But no. Having a premium seat subjects you to stares and a good measure of jealous looks from those who pass by on their way to the economy seats. Or in my case, a haughty glower of disdain from dog man. When he caught sight of me in that oversized luxury seat with lots of legroom, his eye twitched—just a tiny bit. I could hear the sneers of his inner voice say, "Figures." I'd seen that look before. Poor little rich girl.

He shook his head and chuckled before adjusting the strap of the mesh dog carrier on his shoulder and then slugged onward. Back to the backity back back. Who was this guy to judge me anyway? He was probably one of those inconsiderate hobos who didn't clean after their dog did its business. I could just picture him shaking his head all the way down the aisle.

Whatever.

It wasn't my idea to purchase a first-class ticket. My brother bought it, all the while scolding me for waiting too long to book my flight. He'd said something about guaranteeing my seat since

I'd already missed out on a direct flight, it being the holidays and all. But I wasn't about to apologize for Christmas.

I settled in with a small town romance on my Kindle while the plane taxied and took off. A few minutes after we hit cruising altitude I overheard a hushed confrontation between a flight attendant and a lady with a toddler.

"I'm sorry, ma'am. You'll have to take your seat," the flight attendant said. Her hair was pinned in a tight French twist and her navy blue skirt looked like it was cutting off her circulation. An extremely wiggly child in pigtails squirmed in the passenger's arms. She appeared to be training for cirque de soleil the way she was bending backwards.

"It's just she was climbing off my lap. I'll go right back when the seatbelt sign is on."

"We can't allow passengers to walk freely around the cabin. We have to get through with the beverage service."

The tired mom scanned the first-class area, gesturing to the empty seat. "I'll be out of your way in here."

"This area is restricted. I have to ask you to return to your seat."

The poor woman hitched the squirrely little girl on her hip and disappeared down the aisle after the flight attendant drew the curtain. This was followed by silly squeaks and squeals so high-pitched, a coloratura soprano would be jealous. A few people laughed but I figured there were others who didn't appreciate the joyful noises of a toddler.

When the flight attendant returned my way I called her to me. "That woman with the baby. Is she traveling alone?"

She twisted her brows and gave me a confused expression. "Yes, I believe she is, Miss Darcy."

Miss Darcy. This lady knew who I was, or rather, who my brother was. His name was on my itinerary since he paid for the flight. A celebrity brother had its perks even though it was annoying.

"I would like to switch seats with her."

Her confused expression turned to shock. Or she was appalled. I couldn't figure out which. "I....uh...I'll have to ask my supervisor."

"I'm sure it's fine." I gathered my things, which consisted of a small purse and my Kindle. "I'll just pop into the bathroom while you lead her up here. Then you can show me my new seat."

I didn't wait for her response. I took my time in the first-class bathroom, flossing my teeth and re-applying my lip-gloss. By the time I finished, the little girl and the mom were gleefully sharing the seat I vacated with lots of room to wiggle and roam in peace.

I was feeling pretty darn good about my Christmas good deed, smiling to myself as the flight attendant led me toward the rear—until I got there.

"This is you. The middle seat."

Yikes. No wonder the tike couldn't sit still. The seat was tiny and the older woman in the aisle seat hardly tucked in her legs to let me pass. There was approximately three inches between her and the seat in front of her. But the real shocker was the person who occupied the window seat. I first noticed the bag tucked under the seat and a little black nose peeking out from under the folds of mesh. Big, brown eyes regarded me, sorrowfully imploring to be let out—and maybe to jump on me. Again. Reeses and his human stared at me incredulously. The latter, a little more bemused than the other.

"Bored with champagne and caviar?" His elbow was on my armrest.

"What?"

"I saw you in the fancy section. Were you curious how the other half lives? Or did they kick you out?"

I nudged my right elbow, knocking his off the armrest. "Nope. I'm just hoping to get attacked by your dog again."

"Attacked?" He laughed. "Yeah, those doggie kisses are mighty lethal."

Charming.

"How do you know I'm not allergic?"

"If you're allergic, you probably shouldn't have tried to pet Reeses earlier."

"I wasn't trying to pet your...Reeses. I was trying to get through your entourage of jail bait so I could plug in my phone."

At that point Dog Man's lip twitched. I thought at first he was trying to hold back a guilty grin but there was more to it than that. His features spread out to reveal a mouthful of teeth. I'm talking really nice teeth. But that's beside the point. He was laughing at me. Laughing. At me. The nerve—especially after all the trouble he'd caused me. To crown the whole, his little dog considered the laughter an invitation to join the fun because he slipped out of his mesh bag and jumped on his human's lap. No biggie. Just a dog on a plane.

Here's where I feel I should add a little disclaimer. I loved dogs. Adored them actually. I couldn't have pets where I lived, but if I could, I'd have adopted a dog. For the time being, I had to settle for visits to California where I got to snuggle with my brother's cocker spaniel to my heart's content. So I had absolutely nothing against Reeses. But I was a rule follower and I was pretty sure dogs had to stay put in their carriers while in flight. Dog Man didn't seem to care one bit.

"Ya know. If you get caught, they'll issue you a travel ban. I've seen it happen."

"Doubtful."

"Fine." I angled my body away from him the best I could in that tiny seat and plugged my earbuds into the armrest. Weird place for the media controls, but whatever. I'd be laughing my head off once that fierce flight attendant put Dog Man in his place.

But Reeses was swift. It was as though he could sense when someone was coming because he'd jump into his carrier (which was more like a duffle bag) and bury his head under the flap. Then, when the danger passed, he'd leap right back onto Dog Man's lap with his cute little ears perked up.

Unbelievable!

All my efforts to find my happy place were in vain. The lady sitting to my left continued to push the call button. At first I thought she wanted to complain about Reeses, but she only wanted a pillow. Then a blanket. Then when she was told there were no blankets, she wanted the "waitress" to drape napkins over her shoulders. Of course she was a gem compared to the guy. He seemed to consider himself entitled to my armrest. His elbow pressed directly over the media controls, either changing my channel or increasing the volume to deafening levels. Each time I *kindly* asked him to move his elbow, he just said, "Oops." and replaced it there again after a minute. Seriously. What kind of dummy designed those media controls?

My only consolation was the short duration of the flight. Soon we'd be in Chicago where I'd catch my connecting flight to Los Angeles and the Dognamic Duo would go to whichever circus they belonged.

But, oh! Fate was a trickster. Or at least the weather was.

"Ladies and gentlemen, this is your captain speaking..."

3

GEORGIA

The ticketing agent at Fort Dodge Municipal Airport was garnering a little too much amusement at our expense. It was a nightmare scenario out of a Steve Martin movie. Chicago O'Hare runways all slick with black ice. No flights for a couple days out of Fort Dodge, Iowa. But oh, there's a Motel 6 in town with a great continental breakfast. Happy Holidays.

I attempted to reason with the lady one last time while the line behind me grew into a collective frown.

"So you're telling me you can't find *any* flights to LAX? Or at least another airport where I can grab a connecting flight?"

She lifted one brow and peered at me over her reading glasses. "Listen, I already said…this is a municipal airport."

"Yes, but surely they can arrange for some commercial planes to swing by and take all these people where they need to go. Or lots of small planes. It's Christmas."

"I don't know what Polar Vortex means to you folk in L.A. but here in Iowa it means: All. Flights. Grounded."

Honestly I thought polar vortex was some kind of Star Trek thing. But I digress.

"So, when you say all flights grounded, does that pertain to flights going to a warmer climate?"

She exhaled a heavy, punctuated breath. It was a statement in itself, pretty much declaring my idiocy. I was okay with that as long as my questions were answered. She held up her hand and began ticking my options off on her fingers.

"You can accept the hotel and food voucher and wait out the storm."

Tick.

"You can catch the charter bus tomorrow morning into Chicago."

Tick.

"Or...you can try to rent a car.

Tick

"But..." The *but* was accentuated with a scary plosive consonant accompanied by a spray of spit. "...they only keep eight cars in the fleet."

I bolted. Yes, I thanked the lady, but I was running so fast she probably didn't hear me. Eight cars in the fleet. Total? Or eight of each kind? I hoped and prayed I wasn't too late. In retrospect I should have asked where the rental car place was but really, Fort Dodge Municipal Airport, Iowa was more like a library than a transport center. My brother's house was bigger which kind of wasn't a fair comparison because Pemberley was crazy huge.

I wondered as I ran through the carpeted corridors, past Native American wall art, past a life-size plaster statue of a moose, past a museum exhibit of the early aviators, how my day took such a wild turn. At this moment I should have been boarding my second flight to L.A. with a steamy peppermint latte acquired at the Chicago airport Starbucks. I'd be taking my seat, settling in for a lazy five hours in the air before I got to see my brother and his fiancé. Before arriving home for Christmas.

And instead I was rushing through a sad little airport to get one of eight rental cars before people with working phones could snatch them up in the app.

What kind of lunacy was this? First thing first. Rent a car. Then buy a burner phone to call Will. Then...drive to a working airport? I couldn't think that far ahead without my caffeine.

I found the line to the Cheap and Cheerful Car Rental before the blaring yellow sign came into view. There definitely was nothing cheerful about that line. Also, even if the travelers waiting not so patiently were four to a party, eight cars wouldn't be enough to accommodate all those people. My chances of getting out of this place were getting dimmer than the fluorescent lights on the tile ceiling. In my desperation I thought to myself, "Surely one of these nice souls would have room for one more." Then I thought about how my brother would react and tamped that down before the imaginary voice in my head could yell, "Stranger danger." A businessman in an important looking suit glared angrily at his expensive looking watch then shot laser beams toward the front of the line where the clerk attended to a customer. Said customer was most assuredly thinking to himself. "Too bad, suckers. I got here first. Enjoy your lumpy oatmeal tomorrow morning."

Or maybe it was a sweet elderly lady taking the last car so she could see her grandchildren for the holidays. I had to know who to direct my ire towards. So I followed the important businessman's gaze until my vision landed on the lucky jerk renting one of the last cars. Dog Man.

Seriously, my day couldn't have gotten any weirder. There he was, fumbling through his stuff, dropping all the contents of his wallet onto the counter. The cashier shook her head and said something I only caught the tail end of as I drew closer.

"...can't accept cash. Credit cards only." She shrugged as though she couldn't care less and for a split second I felt sorry for Dog Man. Nobody should have to endure the indifference of a tired rental car clerk. Not three days before Christmas. Then I remembered his indifference about my broken phone and a small part of me—the vindictive part—rejoiced at his plight. He looked so pathetic in those jeans that were too worn to be fashionable and a pair of extremely insensible Converse All Stars—also run down. Did this guy not know how to dress for the snow? Reeses' little snout peeked out of the bag on the floor and I only had time to note the flash in his eyes upon spotting me before he unzipped the bag with the force of his body. Yes—unzipped the bag. He bounded to me and jumped so fast, I could only open up my arms to catch him. That took a lot of faith on his part. I could have let him tumble to the floor for all her knew. Instead I found myself with an arm full of energetic Jack Russell Terrier and a face full of doggy kisses. Why me? Was this his secret ploy to get away from his current human? I thought only cats did that.

"Give me ten seconds," Dog Man begged the cashier.

"You got five," she said impatiently.

I was halfway to the counter by the time Mr. Attention Seeker reached me.

"You again," he snarled.

"Can I help it if Reeses likes me better than you?"

"Just give me my dog."

"Ooh," I chirped. "Do I sense a hint of jealousy?"

Something in his features shifted, as though I'd hit a nerve and he narrowed his stare into slits, stepping into my personal space. I could smell the prickly annoyance on him...and I kind of liked it. His face was so close to mine I could bite his nose if I were so inclined. Reeses' doggy ways were beginning to rub off on me.

"Don't flatter yourself, princess. He's just hoping for some caviar to drip from your entitled chin."

"Okay, first of all...ew, and second—"

"Excuse me. Can you two love birds hurry it up?" The guy next in line waved his arms around.

Love birds?

"Sir," the cashier called to Dog Man. "Does your wife have a credit card?"

Ping! I had a light bulb moment. One my over-protective brother would certainly not approve. Dog Man saw it in my eyes and wildly shook his head.

"Oh, no. Nope. She's not my wife." He slipped back to the counter. I still had Reeses.

"Listen, I've got a hundred twenty-eight fifty. That's more than enough for the rental to California." He practically threw all his cash at the clerk. His hands were shaking. This guy had some serious issues.

"Even if we did accept cash, and we don't, that will only afford you one day's rental." The clerk was smiling but I could see the condescending frown under the surface. "Now please. Step aside."

I really couldn't explain what came over me in that moment. Perhaps it was sheer desperation to the point of complete loss of common sense. I didn't know anything about Dog Man other than a superficial assessment of his appearance—however easy on the eyes said appearance was.

"Actually, he's telling the truth." I shot Dog Man a *just follow my lead* sideways glance. His brows scrunched together. I continued as if I didn't notice. "I'm *not* his wife. Yet." I extended my left hand to proudly display the cubic zirconia ring my brother made me wear to fend off would-be suitors. I wasn't kidding about the over-protective bit. "We haven't told my parents yet. We're on our way to California to surprise them. Reeses here helped with the proposal. Didn't you, boy?"

A collective awww came from all the females within

hearing distance and I nuzzled Reeses to drive it home. Good crowd.

"What are you doing?" Dog Man hissed.

"I'm sorry Homer. I forgot you get embarrassed easily." I planted Reeses right in Dog Man's chest.

"My name is not Homer." He glared at me with a heat so intense his chocolate eyes almost turned to ganache. I waved it off to explain to the clerk.

"Oh, I just nicknamed him Homer Simpson because he loves 'dem donuts." I pinched the sweater bulging around Dog Man's waist.

"That's adorable. Do you have a credit card or not?" Such a ball of sunshine, that lady.

"American Express okay?"

My new fake fiancé's eyes went round as I handed the cashier my Platinum card. Sunshine Lady snapped it from my fingers and ran it through the computer at the other end of the counter.

"That was my rental car," Dog Man spat. "You can't just cut in line and steal people's rental cars."

"Cut in line? Are you in fifth grade? Anyway, I'm not stealing your rental. See that man?" I inclined my head to a rather large man with a comb over who was next in line. "For the record, I'm stealing *his* rental because Sunshine Lady over there wasn't giving you any breaks."

"I almost had her."

"No you didn't."

The clerk called me over to finish the transaction so I could go over the rental agreement on a touch screen. Dog Man stormed next to me while I happily checked off all the boxes.

"If it wasn't for Reeses you'd be in the back of the line, princess."

"If it wasn't for Reeses, my phone would be working. So I think we're even."

I tapped away at the screen. Rental insurance? Check.

"May I see your ID sir?" the clerk asked Dog Man.

"What? Why?"

She huffed and did that eye roll thing she was so good at. I wondered if that was a job requirement. "If you plan on doing any of the driving, I'll need your ID."

"Of course he's driving," I said. "I hate to drive." That wasn't exactly true. I loved the freedom of driving where I wanted to go when I wanted. What I couldn't stand was being chauffeured around in a town car when I was in high school. All my friends had sweet rides—convertibles and stuff—but my famous brother had me on a short leash. It was for my protection but still...

"I err... yeah." Dog Man set Reeses back in the case and slipped his license out of his wallet. Sunshine Lady volleyed her eyes between us and chuckled.

"What?" Dog Man and I said in unison.

"You fight like an old married couple," she said, running Dog Man's ID through the reader. "I can always tell the ones who are gonna make it."

We must have had the most ridiculous expressions on our faces as she handed Dog Man his ID. Her tone was almost robotic as she said, "Congratulations on your engagement."

Yep. Weirdest day ever.

4

WYATT

That was a weird turn of events. Not twenty-four hours since I got an exclusive leak from my contact in Los Angeles and next thing I know I was on a plane to chase the story. This could be my big break if I could just get there on time. Now I was sharing a ride in rural Iowa with the prettiest girl I've ever met. Spunky and infuriating, yes. But pretty. A no make-up kind of beautiful with a natural pink to her cheeks and honey locks framing her face. And I had no business looking at her like that. Plus that engagement ring on her finger cost more than I'd make in a year. Definitely too much trouble.

She spent the first twenty minutes looking out the window without uttering a word to me. The silence drove me crazy. So I cranked the radio. She immediately shut it off and crossed her arms.

Alrighty then.

When she finally spoke, I couldn't decide if I was relieved or disappointed she broke the silence.

"I need a burner phone."

"Okay. Next stop, I guess."

"Good."

I continued down the highway, careful to keep my eyes on the road but every few minutes I stole a glance her way—just to see the back of her head, I supposed. Reeses was happy at least, fast asleep on her feet.

"You can use my phone if you want to call whoever was supposed to pick you up at LAX," I offered.

She kind of bristled at the suggestion, as if my cheap Metro phone wasn't good enough for her.

"Nope. It can wait."

More silence. More staring out the window. I wanted to point out to her the weather wasn't my fault—even though she acted like the planes were all grounded because of some evil plan I'd devised. But I settled for civility, reminding myself it was her who got us this car and I'd have to pay her back somehow.

"I suppose I should probably thank you for your unorthodox improv skills back there."

She looked at me for a second and then turned back to the window.

"So...Reeses and I thank you. I'll pay my share of the rental once I get paid from my gig in L.A. And for your phone, too."

That caught her attention. "Gig? You an actor?"

"No way."

"Musician?"

"Nope." I was a little embarrassed to say, so I went with vague. "I'm a writer."

She snorted. "Screenwriter."

I wished. But no.

"Actually, I'm a journalist. Working on a big story."

"Oh? What's the story?"

"That's top secret, I'm afraid."

She repressed a grin. "Okay, Clark Kent."

"Clark Kent, huh?"

"Yeah. You've got that Clark Kent vibe going on. But without the glasses." She swished her fingers around in little circles in my direction.

"So...Superman, then." I wagged my brows.

"Ha. Dream on. Not the looks. Just the fumbling nerdy part."

I had to agree with her on that. But I owned it, so it was okay.

"So do you have a name?" she asked, shifting in her seat to face me better. "Or do I have to continue calling you Dog Man?"

I almost spit out my morning coffee, which would have been really something since I'd consumed that hours ago.

"Dog Man? Hmmm. That's kind of charming. I think I'll stick with that."

She huffed. "Fine."

I half-laughed. Daddy's little princess liked to pout when she didn't get her way. I considered for a brief moment to let her call me Dog Man for the rest of the ride. But I realized the flaw in that. Besides, I didn't know her name either and calling her princess wasn't going to go over well. I was too busy being angry and dazzled by her at the airport to notice when she signed her name. And the rental agreement was in the glove box. What was it about this girl?

"I'm just kidding," I said. "I'm Wyatt."

She raked her eyes over me in open assessment.

"Hmmm. I guess."

"You guess? It's not like I'm giving you a fake name."

"You could be."

My fingers gripped tighter around the steering wheel. "Why would I do that?"

"Because you're a reporter on a top-secret assignment."

Cute. Wild imagination. Maybe a tad delusional.

"You can check the rental agreement in the glove box."

"Nah. I'm good."

"All right. Believe me, don't believe me. I don't care." Then why did it bother me so much? "What's your name, then?"

She hesitated. Maybe thinking up something outrageous. "Georgia."

"Okay, *Georgia*. When we make the next stop we'll exchange IDs and see which one of us is lying."

"NO!" she blurted.

Interesting.

"I mean...I don't like my picture," she quickly added.

So she was vain too. Funny, I didn't have her pegged as vain with that fresh, glowing face. Spoilt and entitled, sure. But not vain. A ping a disappointment shot through me. And why did it matter anyway?

A length of silence descended upon us while we drove down that rural road for the next couple of hours. There was nothing but snow for miles in every direction. I checked the indicators. Almost a full tank of gas. Thank goodness for tiny cars.

We were both flustered and bristled when they'd pulled the Chevy Spark around for us. Georgia's snubby reaction to the tiny economy car was priceless. She stormed into the passenger seat and slammed the door. I was more than happy to 'not so gently' toss her carry-on in the trunk and I sped off without inputting a destination in the GPS. I followed the signs Southbound, just wanting to *literally* get out of Dodge. I figured we could find a more suitable place down the road to go over our travel plans from here on out. But there was nothing. Absolutely nothing but the occasional farmhouse. I was fairly certain we were on a major highway.

Hungry for some snacks, I reached behind my seat for my backpack, only swerving slightly. She flipped out.

"Oh my—sheesh! Are you trying to kill us?"

"Calm down, woman. It was your idea to make me drive."

"Yeah, because I've never driven on icy roads. I thought you'd know how *not* to plow into a snow bank."

Reeses raised his little head and perked up his ears. He volleyed his face toward me, then Georgia, then back to me again and barked once.

"See?" said Georgia. "Your dog agrees with me."

"Nah. He has to do his business. That's his 'I need to pee' bark."

I eventually found a turnout—a spot just off the road where it would be safe to let Reeses out so he could roam around. It was a scenic spot overlooking a lake, now frozen over with ice and snow. A few lonely picnic benches caked in several inches of snow sat just beyond the parking lot. This lakeside rest area was a scenic place even covered in white. I could imagine how beautiful it would be in warmer weather.

"Just open your door and he'll jump out," I said. "I'm going to take some pictures."

I scooped up my backpack and slipped outside into the frigid air. The parking lot was icy and a little slippery under my Converse All Stars.

I heard Georgia shriek in response to the cold before snapping the door shut after letting Reeses out. My little dog hopped along, bouncy as ever, bolting from one spot to another to leave his mark. Animal kingdom, Reeses the dog was here. He was in his element. Really, anywhere he could exert some of that pent-up energy was his element.

I reached in my bag for my most prized possession—the Nikon 8008s I scrimped and saved for and finally purchased when Costco had a sale. It was the only thing of value I owned. I snapped a few shots of the snowy scenery of the frozen lake, the frosty trees. Beautiful. I could sell these photos on Shutterstock. Put my associates degree in photography to good use.

Fifteen minutes passed by. I had some great images. Reeses was still merrily peeing on everything in sight. I heard Georgia call out.

"Can you believe this car has crank windows? Crank!"

"Well roll it back up before you freeze," I cried back.

"I'm already frozen in here without the heater. Can you hurry it up?" She'd put her knit cap back on, strands of hair poking out from underneath. Half her upper body leaned outside the window like Reeses sometimes did on summer truck rides back home. With the fluffy lining of her hooded coat and her gloved hands, she looked just as snuggly and soft.

Wrong thoughts. Bad thoughts. Shove those down.

I replaced my camera's lens cap and carefully nuzzled it in my bag. Just a little road trip, nothing more. Then I'll never see her again. I repeated those words, keeping my head down as I crunched through the snow towards the car. Towards that girl. That maddeningly beautiful girl.

Then she screeched. I threw my head up to see that tiny car sliding on the ice, Georgia halfway out the window. I hurried to get closer but once I set foot on the pavement my shoes slid from under me. I scrambled to get up.

"Pull the emergency brake," I screamed. The car was still on the move, gliding dangerously close to the lake's edge.

"The brake *is* on." She was opening her door.

"Wait!" I knew how this would go down. I wrote an article on it for an online magazine once. They paid me ten bucks. "The door will shut on you if you don't open it wide."

"What?"

"And jump at a forty-five degree angle."

By this time she was perched to jump. "You seriously expect me to do math right now?"

The car was still sliding. I don't know what powers suddenly came over me, but I figure skated on over to her. Scott Hamilton, eat your heart out. The car's front wheels hit the icy lake. Would it hold the weight?

"Jump!"

I'd never seen someone catch so much air. That woman soared through the air like one of those flying squirrels. I got to her just in time to break her fall and we both plummeted to the cold pavement. For a long moment all we could do was breathe. Heavy, spent breaths. Happy to be alive breaths. Faces intoxicatingly close to one another breaths. Georgia's hat was askew which let long whips of hair fall in a curtain around us. Her pillowy lips were right there, just an inch or two from touching mine. I may have lost my hearing for a few seconds. The only sound registering was the thumping of my heart. She smelled of strawberries. Probably her shampoo or body wash. Strawberries in the dead of winter. I'd gone to heaven.

I didn't realize my arms were wound around her until she moved to lift her body off mine. A fierce shade of pink flushed over her cheeks and I had a strong suspicion it wasn't due to the cold.

5

GEORGIA

I couldn't decide if I was mortified, grateful, or all fluttery. Wyatt looked ridiculous slipping and sliding along the icy pavement in those insensible shoes, arms flapping in the wind. Next thing I knew he was under me, a soft barrier from the hard ground. It's like he was kind of heroic but in a fumbling, unlikely sort of way. This close to him, I was arrested by the smallest details. The gold flecks in his eyes, the lush, thick lashes any woman would envy, the small dimple on his left cheek.

"Ummm." It was awkward. Really awkward. And I hoped he didn't have a broken tailbone or something. "Are you okay?"

He blinked and sucked in a breath. "I think."

A cold dog nose got into my face, sniffing and licking, awakening me from the temporary insanity in which I almost found Wyatt attractive. I pushed off from his chest and rolled over, sitting up to look at the car.

"It stopped sliding. Do you think we could back it up?"

Wyatt groaned as he sat up. That tailbone was going to bruise for sure. "Oh." He sounded surprised and hopeful. "Maybe we'll be lucky."

Now, I'm not one to put too much stock into such things, but when a chronically unlucky person tempts fate, bad things happen. I was beginning to think bad luck followed Wyatt everywhere he went. For as soon as he uttered those words, the ice cracked and the front end of our little rental car sank into the lake.

We stared at it. Our jaws hung down. There were no words. This could not be happening. A fierce heat spread out from my chest and reached the top of my head, building pressure with each pulse beat in my temples. I felt my eyes narrow into precisely pointy death rays and I turned my head ever so slowly to direct them at the walking disaster sitting next to me. I would have remained in that position indefinitely on the off chance those death rays might actually work—if I could only concentrate enough. But my butt was cold and wet, not to mention the car sinking in the lake, and I wasn't interested in concentrating on Wyatt more than I ought.

TWO HOURS later we were warming ourselves in a greasy spoon down the street from the auto shop where the rental car was towed. Boonybushes, Nebraska. Population: eleven.

I did *not* kill Wyatt. I only made him wish I had.

The tow truck driver (whose name escaped me) owned and ran the auto shop, was the only mechanic, and sold his wife's homemade jams in the front office. One could say he was a true renaissance man.

"How long did he say it would be?" I asked Wyatt as I bit into a fry. I just wanted to get back on the road and out of that one-horse town.

"I dunno. But now would be a good time to call whoever's going to pick you up at LAX." He slid his phone across the table.

It was completely scuffed up, the screen so cracked it belonged on the backside of a plumber. I picked it up and wondered at the oddity of this guy. Did he make a habit of walking under ladders and crossing by black cats? I felt like saying, "You see Wyatt? *This* is why we can't have nice things."

I ran my finger over the screen, remembering my shattered phone. That was the least of my worries at the moment. It seemed so long ago. Funny how drastically my day had gone bonkers.

The home screen was locked.

"What's your password?"

Wyatt hesitated. He'd just taken a bite from his burger. Barbecue sauce dripped down his hands. He held up a finger while he swallowed.

"C."

I pressed C.

"A."

"Okay." I pressed the A.

"L-L."

"Gotcha."

"M." A twinkle in his eyes. "O-M."

I punched it in. "Call Mom? That's some password."

He took a sip of Coke. "A gentle reminder. I let the day get away from me sometimes."

"Have you called her yet today?" I tapped on the dial pad.

He nodded, stealing one of my fries. "Did this morning."

"Hey!" I slapped his hand. "I'm rationing those."

"You can have one of my onion rings," he said sheepishly.

I stared at the phone. Crack in the screen. Crack in the universe. Prisoner Zero has escaped.

"Oh no!"

"It's just a French fry." He held out an onion ring for me.

"No, that's not it." I snatched the onion ring and set in on my plate to enjoy later. "I don't have any numbers memorized. How am I going to call my brother?"

Wyatt twisted his features in thought. "Online white pages?"

"Is that a thing?"

He shrugged.

"Anyway, he'd be unlisted." If it were that easy to find Will Darcy's phone number, he'd get calls from fan girls nonstop.

"Is he on Facebook or something?" Wyatt suggested. "You could direct message him."

My brother's idea of social media was to let someone run an official fan page. However...

"I know what I can do." I tapped away to the search engine and found The Gardiner Theatre's website. I could leave a message for Stella. She was a close family friend. She could get me through to my brother. It was the only thing I could think of. I was surprised to find the messaging system had a staff directory and was patched right through to Stella's office. Interesting how she was probably more famous than my brother yet so accessible. Her chirpy British accent greeted me on her recorded voicemail.

"Stella. It's me Georgia. Listen, my plane was snowed in and I need to get ahold of Wi—" I stopped myself from using my brother's real name. "Billy. Trying to get ahold of my brother Billy. Long story, my phone broke. I'm calling from a friend's phone." I noticed Wyatt's lip twitch just then. "Give...*Billy* this number please." I rattled off Wyatt's number with his help and hung up, just a little despondent. What were the chances Stella would go into the theatre a few days before Christmas? They had a Holiday Show but she didn't need to be there for that. I handed the phone back.

"Anyone...else you'd like to try?" asked Wyatt.

"Nope."

He shrugged and set his phone next to his plate. "So, I was thinking. We should chart a course the rest of the way to LA. Find the route with the least snow."

"What are you talking about? We only need to get to an airport. Preferably one with a working runway."

Wyatt stilled. Apparently that idea never crossed his mind. "Oh. I...I don't have enough for another plane ticket."

"Didn't you get your travel voucher? The airline owes us."

"Uh, no. I ran straight to the car rentals."

This guy. Seriously.

"Well, I'm sure your name is on a list. Just show your I.D." I took a bite of my club sandwich. "This needs avocado."

Wyatt nodded. "I'm sure you're right. I'm just going to go check on Reeses." He slid out of the booth taking a piece of bacon with him. The restaurant manager let us keep the dog tied up in the vestibule. Wyatt had set his coat on a bench and Reeses made himself comfortable, only perking up for some belly rubs every time a customer walked in.

The waitress came by to refill my water. "What's your dog's name?"

He wasn't *my* dog, but I didn't feel like correcting her. "Reeses."

"Awww. That's cute. Like a sweet little peanut butter cup. Did you name him or did your boyfriend?"

"Boyfriend?"

Her gaze flickered to my fake diamond ring. "Sorry. Husband." She tossed her head around to look at Wyatt. "I sure wish I had a fella that had eyes for me the way that man looks at you. He ain't goin' nowhere, darlin'. It's written on his face plain as day. You're one lucky gal." She winked and fluttered away. She was cute but her unsolicited advice was way off. Did I look like I cared if my man went anywhere? Not that Wyatt was my man or anything.

He returned with a bright smile, that dimple making another appearance amid his afternoon scruff.

Written on his face, huh? Balderdash.

We ate in silence for some time, stealing food off one another's plates. That diner really rocked those onion rings. Wyatt checked his phone every few minutes to see if the mechanic had called. It was getting late and once the sun set, the roads would get icier. But I had to get to L.A. even if that meant taking a red-eye.

After a while I excused myself to the single-stall restroom. I looked into the mirror while washing my hands, the words of that waitress repeating in my mind. *The way that man looks at you.* Was my face telling a story just because I thought my road trip companion was kinda handsome? Did I notice the defined biceps peeking out of his t-shirt sleeve? Or the dusting of dark hair along his rugged forearms? Or those thick, calloused fingertips?

Maybe.

For a split second, right after he caught me, there was a spark. Just a teeny tiny ember. Probably brought on by the position we found ourselves in, and partly because he sort of saved me. In that minuscule moment, a thousand thoughts ran through my head. That maybe I wasn't as damaged as before. That I didn't have to live my life in fear. That I could trust again.

But then the rental car took a nosedive and I decided trust was overrated.

"Get over yourself, Georgie," I told my reflection. "It's just the onion rings talking."

I tapped my toe and sang along to the Christmas music piped into the bathroom. It was the instrumental version of *Sleigh Bells* but I considered it my own personal orchestra as I combed my fingers through my hair to build up courage to get out there and act casual in front of Wyatt.

Giddyup let's go.

Fueled with confidence, I reached for the doorknob and turned the lock. The door didn't budge. Had I forgotten to lock it that whole time only to just lock it now? I switched it back. The knob didn't turn this time. Back again. The knob turned but the door wouldn't open. I pulled and jiggled and pulled some more. Nothing.

I scanned the whole door. Maybe there was a latch somewhere? Nope no latch. That's when panic set in. I could be stuck in this bathroom indefinitely. I pounded the door and cried out. "Help. I can't get out." This was a new low for me. More pounding. "Hello? Anybody?"

It was no use. The ladies room was at the end of a long hallway and there was no way anybody could hear me over the jolly holiday music. It was *The Nightmare Before Christmas* toilet edition. Who knew what magical land that door would lead to next? Was the Oogie Boogie Man on the other side?

I didn't let up, pounding and calling out relentlessly. Surely someone would come along eventually. I noticed several other women in the diner. At least one of them would have to pee soon.

Several minutes passed. It could have been three. It could have been twenty. Hard to tell. I'd almost given up, my forehead pressed against the door, only a feeble wish holding me there.

A *tap tap tap* jolted me. "Honey, are you in there?" It was the waitress. A jiggle of the doorknob.

"Yes!" I cried. Jubilate Deo. "I'm stuck in here."

"Don't you worry, darlin'. This happens all the time."

All the time? Then why wasn't there a warning on the door or something?

"You see that big piece of wood in the corner there?"

I turned. A beveled plank rested against the wall behind the sink.

"Yeah."

"Wedge that under the door."

I followed her instructions.

"Now kick it in until it lifts the door an inch or two."

I kicked that sucker.

"Now what?"

"Stand outta the way."

Next thing I know, the door's flying open. The waitress grinned at me and slapped her hip.

"Strongest part of my body," she said.

"Thank you."

"No worries. Most folks around here know how to deal with that ol' door. When I saw your hubby sittin' all by his lonesome for a long time, I figured where you'd gone off to."

How very observant. I made a mental note to leave a huge tip.

"Why doesn't the owner just fix the door?"

She shrugged one shoulder as we moved down the hallway. "Just one of many things to fix around here, I guess."

I followed her into the dining area and thanked her again as she forked in the opposite direction. When I reached my booth, Wyatt was on the phone, talking animatedly with his hands and smiling like a goon. I wondered who he was talking to. A girlfriend? Maybe he followed his own advice and called his mom. I sank onto the cushion. Did he even notice I'd been gone?

Wyatt laughed. "Yeah, I couldn't believe it either. All our luggage was in the trunk. Small miracles."

A pause while the person on the other end asked a question.

"Well, I hope the guy can fix it. I don't know about mechanical stuff."

He nodded, listening in the phone.

"You got it, man. Anyway, Georgia just sat down so I'm going to pass the phone to her, but it was cool chatting with you, Billy. I'll make sure she gets home safely. Okay. Bye."

Wyatt passed the phone. What on earth?

"Hello?"

"Who the heck is that bozo?" Will barked on the other end. "He wouldn't shut up. Are you okay?"

"Yeah, I'm fine."

"He sounded a whole lotta crazy. You're in Iowa?"

"I think this is Nebraska. But yeah. It's been crazy." I glanced at Wyatt. He had his eyes on the dessert menu card.

"You just stay put. I'm coming to get you." There was urgency in Will's voice.

"No way. I'm fine. You get ready for your big day. I'll be there soon."

"I don't like the idea of you traveling with that guy. You don't even know him, George."

"It's just until we reach a major airport. Don't get all action hero on me. I'm a big girl."

He sighed heavily. "You sound like Beth."

"That's why you love us both so much. Text me Bing's number and I'll call him when I have an ETA."

Bing was my brother's best man. He and his girlfriend Jane lived in Manhattan, not too far from me. Both of them had awesome Broadway gigs but were already in California for the wedding.

"You should have flown out with Bing and Jane a week ago."

"You know why I couldn't do that."

He was silent for a long moment. Probably conjuring up all sorts of scenarios. I knew he was only trying to protect me. But he was getting married and he had his wife to think of now.

"I'll check in with you every few hours. Will that make you feel better?"

"No. I want a tracking device on that man."

"I'll see what I can do. Bye."

Will grunted. I took that as goodbye and ended the call. Wyatt looked up from the dessert menu completely oblivious.

"Billy seems like a nice guy."

Yeah. If you only knew what he thought about you, pal.

6
———
WYATT

As I stood in Al's Auto Repair, watching Georgia's face become increasingly redder, I scolded myself for not paying closer attention to what the mechanic said when he towed the car. Georgia's chin dimpled under the pressure of her clenched jaw and her cute little booted foot tapped impatiently as Al explained why he couldn't do any repairs.

"I don't understand. You said these things could sometimes be fixed."

"The operative word there is sometimes," said Al. "But even if I drain the intake manifold and the combustion chamber, I'd still need to disconnect the fuel injectors and crank the engine over. Maybe then the starter would have enough torque to fling all the standing water from the spark plugs. Then, if the water reached the axle differential..." He scratched his chin, thinking about the various scenarios. It was Greek to me. I should have paid closer attention in my high school shop class instead of daydreaming about poetry.

As Al continued to talk, and boy could that guy talk, I realized why Georgia and I tuned him out earlier. His jargon went right over her head and I was too distracted by her pink cheeks and spunky mannerisms. She may not have gotten everything he said, but she perched her eyebrows high and nodded as if to say, "Make it so." Jean Luc Picard style.

That's when we left for the diner.

Georgia was cute as a button but she was a spitfire when she let herself get all riled up. Something stirred in me that wasn't all that unpleasant. I could tell by the way her fists clenched while Al rattled on—there was a tempest brewing in that pint-sized figure of hers and one way or another, she'd find a way to land the blame on me.

I swallowed that down with a hard lump in my throat. No matter how pretty, that girl was spoilt. Poor little rich girl accustomed to getting her way. I'd been there, done that, thank you very much. And got my heart stomped on.

Besides—Georgia had a huge rock on her finger. Some lucky son of a monkey would miss her tonight.

"And even if I can get the thing to start, it's still a rental and has to go back to..." he glanced at the license plate frame, reading, "Cheap and Cheerful Car Rental. Sorry. Those are the rules."

Georgia threw me a pointed look, like I was supposed to do something manly. To somehow convince this guy to fix our rental car. I cleared my throat and straightened to make myself appear taller.

"So what you're saying here is—under the right circumstances, the car is fixable," I said with my best Robert De Niro stare.

"In theory, yeah."

"And with a little incentive, you might be convinced to, ya know, help us out?" I winked for good measure. I was talking big. It felt kinda cool. I didn't have money to bribe the guy or anything. Pesky details.

Al crossed his arms and studied Georgia and me. She might

have been batting her eyes or giving him the pout. A trick right out of Reeses' playbook.

Al rolled his tongue around in his cheek—the wheels turning in that head of his. He held all the cards. Mechanics always do. The tension was so high I felt like a contestant on a game show.

After some thought, he finally said, "I'll help you out."

Georgia let out a heavy sigh. She'd been holding her breath that whole time. "Thank you so so so so much."

Al held up a finger.

"I'll let you two stay the night here in my shop and in the morning I'll drive you to the bus station."

"Wait. What?" Georgia cried. "The bus station? Why?"

"Cause I imagine you'll need another car," he countered. "And there ain't no Cheap and Cheerful Car Rental or *any* car rental in this town. You'll have to take the bus to the next county."

Georgia bristled, giving me the side eye like I hadn't tried hard enough to convince this guy to break the rules.

"Can't we go right now?" she blurted.

Al did that thing with his jaw—kind of a half-smirk tradesmen do when particularly annoyed.

"Listen. My youngest son has a Christmas pageant in ten minutes. He's the Star of Bethlehem. He's real excited. If I'm not there on time, my wife will serve my head with the figgy pudding." He looked at me just then and gave me a knowing nod. "You'll understand in about five years, man."

He shrugged on his winter coat. "There's water and snacks in the fridge and help yourself to a jar of my wife's gooseberry jam. It's real good. See ya in the morning."

Georgia touched his arm to stop him before he could leave. "Sir. Please." *Sir?*

"Where are we supposed to sleep?"

Al inclined his head towards the office. "There's a couch in the waiting area. I'll keep the heat on for ya'll."

Georgia and I both stared at the door as the mechanic disappeared through it, clicking it shut. The clank echoed from the outer door as he bolted the lock. Georgia turned her death stare at me again. The same one she'd used when the car sank in the lake.

"I hate you."

"Is this a new development? Or..." I grinned at her. Yeah, she was mad, but there was a playfulness to it. Plus, I loved that incandescent glow in her cheeks when she got all worked up.

She's engaged, man. Hands off.

"Ya know," I said in the most chipper way I could. "We're lucky that guy came by with his tow truck when he did. We could still be out there in that roadside parking lot freezing our butts off. I'd say it's a Christmas miracle."

"A Christmas miracle? We're spending the night in a greasy auto shop instead of a warm bed. How is *this* a Christmas miracle?" She waved her hand around at all the tools and equipment.

"Um...we'll have a screwdriver if we need one."

She rolled her eyes and went off to explore the back of the shop, the offices, and the bathroom. When she came back, the dent between her brows was decidedly more pronounced. "Have you seen that bathroom? The toilet seat is cracked. And the *one* couch in the office has some questionable stains." She crossed her arms. "I'm not sleeping here."

"Okay, okay. We'll find a motel. But we need to be back here on time to catch a ride to the bus station." I began a search on my phone. Hotels in... "What town is this?"

"We don't need to get a ride with Franz. Just order an Uber." Things were so easy for this woman in her charmed life. Well I had news for her.

"I don't think there's Uber in this tiny town. And his name isn't Franz."

I was able to pull up Maps on my phone. According to the GPS, the closest Motel was thirty miles away. Probably where the bus would take us the next morning. I searched for a bus schedule. It was non-existent. Plus it was dark and getting biting cold outside. No way was I going out there. I packed for California weather. And I had a feeling everything closed early in these parts.

Her features hardened. "Surely *'Not Franz '* could have directed us to the nearest hotel." She used finger quotes. "Or maybe there's an Air B&B close by."

"It's Al, and I'm pretty sure this auto shop is the closest we're going to get to an Air B&B." I handed her my phone. "Take a look."

She snatched it from me and started tapping away. Her little tongue peeked out the corner of her mouth when she was concentrating on something. I'd noticed that earlier when she was examining the menu at the diner.

Heaven help me. This was going to be a long night.

7

WYATT

I decided to do some exploring of my own. There really was a huge crack on the toilet seat—but guys don't generally mind those things. The stain on the couch was a dark red. It looked like a homicide scene although it was probably only spilled punch or ketchup or something. Al did have small children after all. There was a photo in a picture frame on his desk. A simply dressed slender woman stared back at me with two boys on either side of her. One was about seven. The other couldn't have been more than five. The little one must have been the son in the Christmas pageant. Both boys had mischievous expressions. But the woman had an easy smile. The sort of look on her face that showed she was in complete control of those two rug rats. And in her arms was a baby bundled in a pink blanket. Something pinged inside me. Al had everything right there in that photo. He was a blessed man.

When I returned to the shop I found Georgia in the driver's seat of a vintage Mustang. It was in pristine condition—a robin egg blue with white trim. It was gorgeous and was even more perfect with a beautiful woman behind the wheel. Except Georgia's eyes were puffy like she'd been crying and her adorable little nose was blemished with red splotches. When she noticed me approach her, she sucked in a hearty breath and put on a brave face. It was just a glimpse but I knew just then. She was a person who knew how to wear a mask. Underneath all that entitled Daddy's Girl bologna was a mystery I intended to solve. Perhaps I had it in me to be an investigative reporter after all.

"That's a nice ride, isn't it?" I said, sweeping my gaze over the Mustang.

She wrapped her fingers around the steering wheel. "Sure is."

"You ever drive a car like this?"

A shadow crossed her features. "No. I can't drive a stick."

"Oh. Maybe I can teach you."

Her brows shot up. "Right now?"

"No." I laughed. "It's a thousand degrees below zero out there. And I'm not in the mood to go to jail for grand theft auto."

"They might have better bathrooms in jail," she joked.

I laughed, peeking my head inside. Reeses was sitting comfortably on her lap, his fuzzy ears perking up at the sound of my voice. He didn't move, though. Usually he was at my feet all the time. But he seemed to like Georgia. She stroked her fingers into the soft fur under his collar. He loved to get scratches there.

"Pop the trunk," I suggested. There was a Native American blanket draped along the backseat and I hoped there were more of those in the trunk. Al left the heater on in the shop, but it was nowhere near cozy. Georgia took a minute to find the lever but eventually found it. When I lifted the lid it was like Christmas came early.

"I found the mother load," I exclaimed. There was a neat pile of folded Native American blankets in the trunk as well as several pairs of moccasins and various leather goods. All hand made. "Whoever owns this car probably sells this stuff at pow wows. Oh wait. I found his price list. Dang, that's dirt cheap."

I scooped up a few blankets and two pairs of moccasins tossing Georgia the smaller pair as I slid into the passenger side of the car. Georgia ran her hand along the fur lining of the shoe. Reeses sniffed it suspiciously.

"I can't just take someone's stuff," she said.

"It's just for the night. Unless you'd rather freeze." I kicked off my converse and sank my chilled feet inside the soft, pillowy moccasin. "Ah. This is nice. It's like a hug for my feet." I unfolded one of the blankets and covered my legs. It was almost like camping.

Georgia stared at the moccasins and bit her bottom lip. After a full minute she passed Reeses to me and took off her boots, lifting her legs on the bench seat between us. She wiggled her toes with apparent relief, pointing and flexing them. When she extended her toes, they brushed momentarily on my leg and I smiled inwardly at her red and white striped socks with dancing elves stitched in. The heavy blanket over my lap provided a cushioned barrier, but the gentle pressure of her small feet shot awareness through me just the same.

When she finally slipped on the moccasins, she sighed.

I nodded knowingly. "Right?"

"Yeah," she said, her face transformed. "They *are* like feet hugs, aren't they? I'm buying these."

Feet hugs. She looked huggable all over. I shifted my vision elsewhere. Anywhere but on Georgia. I was comfortable and cozy under the blanket, but if I had to sleep on the murder couch to get my mind off the pretty girl a couple feet away, I'd do whatever it took.

Something shiny caught my eye. The keys were in the ignition. They were really trusting at this place.

"Should we put on some tunes?" I reached over and

switched on the auxiliary power before getting a reply. A song came on I didn't recognize. Georgia winced. I remembered her shutting off the car radio earlier. What did she have against good 'ol honky-tonk?

"What? Don't you like music?"

"I like music if it's done well," she answered.

"Okay. Give me an example."

She didn't hesitate. "Pachelbel, Mozart, Hayden...Chopin."

"Really? I was not expecting that." I turned the knob on the radio to change the channel. Most of it was static, some commercials, and more static again. "Maybe we'll get lucky and find an after-hours classical station," I said.

A smile cracked on her pretty lips and she leaned closer to me to give Reeses a nice scratch. That strawberry shampoo or lotion she used hit my senses. I breathed it in ever so covertly. Didn't want her to think I was a weirdo or anything.

"There! Go back," she chirped. "That's Elvis."

I turned the knob back. Sure enough, it was *Blue Christmas*.

"How did you catch that?"

She smiled smugly. "I have a good ear."

"A far cry from Bach or Tchaikovsky," I mused.

"It's Elvis *and* Christmas. Classical music."

We listened for a bit, swaying where we sat. The lyrics reminded me of how alone I'd be this Christmas. The first away from my folks. Then I watched her face. She had a sweetheart back in New York or was he in LA? And she was stuck with me in Nowhere's Ville, Nebraska with no phone to call him—thanks to me.

"Do you miss him?"

"Hmmm?" She was too into the music. "Elvis?"

"Uh, no." I shook my head. So silly, this one. "Your boyfriend or...fiancée or whatever."

She stopped swaying and stared at me blankly. "Fiancée? I never said I had a fiancée."

I gestured to her left hand. "It's a little obvious with a year's salary in diamonds on your ring finger."

She glanced at the ring then back at me and laughed. She had a sweet laugh. It made my heart swell—which I would have liked if I wasn't so utterly confused. Did she think I was funny? I wasn't trying to be funny. I could be so much funnier. At least, she might think I was if she was into dad humor. I was full of corny jokes.

"It's fake," she said on a sigh. "My brother makes me wear it to keep the men away."

Fake. The ring was fake?

"Y-y-you...I mean...uh." Yes. I could speak English. "It doesn't look fake. It looks very real." She was single. The ring was fake. I was in real trouble.

"Well, my brother gave it to me so it must be fake. He's so overbearing. It's annoying."

"Billy? He seemed nice over the phone."

"Ha! You don't know him. He thinks jerky guys will see a ring on my finger and leave me alone. But only the nice guys really notice it. Like you."

"I...errr...you think I'm a nice guy?" Because *that* was what I decided to focus on. *Dork.*

"I think so." Her eyes widened. "You're not a psycho killer or anything are you? I'm an idiot."

"No! You're not an idiot."

"I'm naive."

"I don't know about that." If she was, it was a good look on her. It was refreshing. "There's nothing wrong with trusting people. It's a good quality."

"Really?"

"Definitely." I ticked a brow. "And I'm not a psycho killer. I've had so many opportunities already, Clarice."

She laughed. "Quid pro quo, doctor."

Then a commercial came on and we listened quietly as though it was the most interesting snippet of entertainment in the world. It was a child's voice inviting the surrounding counties to a living nativity at some church. He played the drummer boy apparently. That made Georgia smile. Then she turned her gaze back to me.

"So what about you?"

"Me?"

She giggled. "Yeah. Any girlfriend or...fiancée?

Ha. Hardly.

"Uh, no thank you."

"No thank you? Why?"

"No reason. I'm just super busy, that's all."

She snorted. "I don't buy it. Cute guy like you. There's a story in there somewhere."

"Perhaps." I grinned. It was a goofy grin. The kind that made me grateful to have had braces. Otherwise it would have been a creepy grin.

Her ring was fake. I was still stuck on that. And she thought I was cute.

The commercials ended and the music resumed with *Rockin' Around the Christmas Tree.* Georgia bounced in her seat.

"This is such a bop." She turned up the volume. Loud. "Come on."

She opened her door.

"Where are we going?" I asked.

"Just come on. Let's dance." She leaped out of the car and danced her way to an open space of the garage. Reeses jumped out after her and hopped on his hind legs to join in, wagging his tail. He was a pretty awesome dog. He could do almost any trick. And he loved to dance.

Georgia rocked out, so carefree and sparkling. She was radiant—the way she smiled at Reeses, mirroring his movements. The way she sang along and flung her hair around. There was something magnetic about her, how the air crackled around her. And I was just shards of metal unable to resist the pull.

I threw off the blanket from my lap and sprang into action. Muscle memory took over as I wrapped my hand around Georgia's small fingers, pulling her in to me. It was a simple Lindy Hop sequence. *One, two, rock step, one, two, rock step.* She fell right into rhythm with me. Her delicate hand landed on my shoulder, and I grazed my free hand around her waist.

Her eyes shimmered with surprise—delighted I knew how to swing dance. Most guys didn't bother learning to dance at all. But my mom and dad were big in the swing-dancing scene, taking me and my sister along with them to competitions—and now it was ingrained in me. I twirled Georgia a few times, leading her out then bringing her back with a gentle tug. She followed well. A lot of ladies would try to lead or were too stiff. But Georgia seemed to respond to the light pressure of my hands, spinning out, rocking back, and then again into my arms. Her entire face was a smile—heck—her whole body was. I couldn't remember the last time I had so much fun.

The saxophone wailed the upbeat musical interlude and we were really flying by now. That's when I decided to go for an aerial. She seemed into it. I gave her the signal—an eyebrow wag along with a pronounced nod. Any swing dancer would recognize the nod. The eyebrow thing was just something I added myself. She raised her brows in response. She was ready.

I decided on the Cherry Drop Dip—one of my favorites. I did the pivot thing to start us off; the classic move to signal my partner into position. All she had to do was lock her arm and keep her core solid. My right leg swung around, guiding her behind me. She was right there, so responsive. So I went for it. I pumped my hip, lifting her off the floor. She was up with a little squeal. So cute. Adrenaline shot through me and maybe I got a little too enthusiastic. Or maybe she wasn't expecting me to flip her around. I wasn't really sure what happened in those three seconds when I bumped Georgia off my right hip and swung her around over my left leg. Her legs flailed up and bounced off my back. Her arms wiggled under my hold. And my leg wobbled—the leg supporting Georgia's weight. She teetered, poised to fall, and although the floor wasn't greasy in that area of the auto shop, it couldn't have been all that clean. So I abandoned all form and grabbed her. I wasn't about that flashy dance move at this point. My only thought was not to let her fall —*again*. At least this time we weren't on icy ground.

I pulled her into me, straightening our bodies into an upright position. Disaster averted. And she was so close. Our noses almost touching. Her eyes, huge pools of maple syrup shined at me, blinking. I could make out every lash—long, feathery fringe brushing against her brows as she gazed at me.

What was that expression? Surprise? Whimsy? Desire?

I zeroed in on her lips. They were parted ever so slightly. And dang! This girl had kissable lips. I could get lost in the softness of them. I could nuzzle right in there and wrap myself up for a long winter's nap.

Not that there would be any napping involved.

Then she smiled softly and I got spooked or something because I jumped back. Reeses yelped. Did I step on his paw? I stumbled to right myself, tripping over the fluffy moccasins on my feet. Reeses leapt into Georgia's arms to avoid my backward trajectory. I did that thing with my arms to find my balance, but that only made things worse when my body hit a work shelf.

The thing was made of a flimsy aluminum. Really, it was a wonder it could hold anything at all because as I fell to the floor, grasping for anything to break my fall, the whole shelving unit came crashing down on me. And all the mechanicky stuff on the shelves came tumbling down with it.

8

GEORGIA

The more time I spent with this Wyatt guy, the more I was convinced he was Charlie Brown in the flesh. I'd never met anyone with worse luck. And what a klutz! He did dance well, though. That was nice. But outside of doing the boogie woogie, he was a walking disaster.

"Are you all right?" I went to reach for him just as a box of washers fell on his head.

"Ow." He winced, but at least didn't seem too damaged. Reeses leapt from my arms to comfort him. "Not now, doggie."

Wyatt peeled himself off the floor and assessed the mess. "This will be fun to clean up."

"I'll help you," I offered.

He gave me a sheepish grin rubbing his head. "Actually, could you check if there's an ice pack somewhere?"

"Ice pack. Got it."

I hurried to the office where I found the first aid kit. Just Band-Aids and a half-used tube of Neosporin. Then I looked in the freezer. There were plenty of Hungry Man dinners but no ice pack.

"Welp. I guess this will have to do."

I grabbed the frozen dinner and snagged a couple of ginger ales from the fridge. This was a well-stocked refrigerator. A package of Italian salami and cheese taunted me. I took that, too.

I got back to the garage to find Wyatt and Reeses in the Mustang, snug under one of the blankets. I slipped in to join them.

"This is all I could find," I said, handing him the frozen dinner. He accepted it with a smile and placed it on his head.

"I'm so embarrassed."

"Don't be. At least it wasn't an audience of hundreds. Here." I handed him a ginger ale.

"Thanks." He rested the can on the other side of his head.

"That's for drinking."

"Yeah, but I don't have a free hand." He winked. "Salisbury steak dinner and a soda. I'm all set."

"Well when you're done heating it up with your head I'll pop it in the microwave for you," I joked.

He chuckled. I tore open the salami and cheese pack and we recounted his ridiculous fall while we nibbled. I fed him his first few bites before he abandoned his makeshift ice pack so he could use his hands.

I shut off the radio to save the car's battery and we talked for a long time about Christmas traditions. He told me about making minced meat empanadas with his mom (well, less making them and more eating them) and I told him about our California snowball fights which were really just an excuse to throw crumpled up wrapping paper at each other.

We finished our snack and moved on to dessert. Candy canes and some cookies Wyatt had in his backpack. We gobbled those up. Then he insisted I at least text my brother to give him peace of mind. Wyatt already had Will's number saved as 'Billy' in his phone's contacts. So I sent a quick text while Wyatt took Reeses out and then I set the phone to silent.

They weren't gone long. Even Reeses was done with the cold.

"Brrr." Wyatt stretched his feet on the dash. "You know what sounds really good right now?"

"An antacid?" I was beginning to regret all that salami.

"Nope. A warm, cozy fire and a mug of hot cocoa."

Ah, yeah. That did sound nice. I became more aware of the chill inside the garage and tucked my blanket under my chin. Even with the central heat on, the place lacked the insulation to keep it in.

"Mmmm. That'll be something to look forward to when we get to California."

He laughed. "I doubt the amenities are that snug at the Motel 9."

"Oh. I guess not."

I was on the verge of inviting him to come visit while in Los Angeles but then I thought better of it. My brother guarded his privacy.

Instead I asked, "What did you say you're doing in L.A. on Christmas? Some top secret news story?"

He hesitated. "Yeeeah."

"Is it political?"

"Can't say."

"Papal visit?"

He laughed. "No. Kinda the opposite."

"Hmmm." I scrunched my brows together. What could it be?

"Okay. I can tell you this."

I perked up and Reeses took the opportunity to nuzzle under my arm.

"All I can say is that it's an exclusive. There's a good chance the story hasn't leaked. If I get this, I hold all the cards. It's a good payday."

"So if it's such a secret story, how did you learn about it?"

"I know a guy."

I snorted. "Riiiight."

"Whatever." Wyatt shrugged and reached in his bag for more snacks. "Snickers?"

"No thanks." My tummy couldn't handle any more junk food.

Wyatt noshed on his candy bar. Not a care in the world.

"What about you?" he asked between bites.

"Me? I'm just going home for Christmas. That's all. Nothing exciting. No top secret missions or anything." Did I sound too obvious? I probably did.

"No, I mean. What do you do? Back in New York?" He popped the rest of the candy bar into his mouth. It was more than half. He watched me, waiting for my reply while laboring to chew the huge bite of peanuts, chocolate and nougat.

My brother liked to warn me not to give people too much information. Part of it was a little excessive even for a celebrity. But part of it was founded in the very real fear someone might try to take advantage of me again. So I went with vague.

"I'm a student."

I didn't say I studied classical piano at Juilliard, or that just the night before I played a private concert for the Governor of New York and several senators. That was why I had to cut my trip so close to Christmas.

I scratched Reeses, trying to think of a way to change the subject before Wyatt could swallow that big chunk of chocolate.

"I have a dog back home. In California."

His brows rose.

"Lady. She's an English Cocker."

Technically Lady was my brother's dog but she was just as devoted to me. She was the best dog in the world. I ran my finger on Reeses' snout. "I think Reeses will like her."

Wyatt smiled, his teeth covered in chocolate. "If she's as sweet as her human, he won't be able to resist her."

9

GEORGIA

I had a headache, there was a distinct jabby feeling in my back, and my neck was so stiff I thought my head would snap off. Ah, the joyous pleasure of sleeping in a car.

I'd dozed off after a long, easy conversation with Wyatt. He had a lot of fun stories growing up in a large family. He reminisced about summers spent entirely in swim trunks eating apricots straight from the tree. And about the rope swing his grandfather tied on the branch of a sturdy oak in their yard. How he'd swing and swing for hours pretending to be a superhero, pushing off from the trunk to spin in wide circles. It seemed like a beautifully simple childhood. So different from mine. A whole other planet than the stark realities of Tinseltown, growing up the daughter and sister of two huge film stars. The busy schedules, the endless train of people wanting this and that. Superficial friendships. Hired drivers to take me to school. The gold-digging stepmother who singlehandedly sent my dad to an early grave. And the only thing my brother and I had left of our parents—a giant mansion. The big, lonely prison for two when Will shut the world away to protect me.

I twisted the ring on my finger. One last feeble attempt of my brother to keep the big bad wolf away from his little sister.

"Rise and shine, Georgia Peach."

I looked over to find Wyatt folding those Native American blankets on the hood of the Mustang.

"Don't worry. I slept in the backseat. Your honor is intact, milady."

"Okay. Thanks?" Funny, the thought never crossed my mind. I opened the car door and crawled out.

"Oh, and your brother called. I gave him an update and promised I'd get you home for Christmas. He didn't say much. He's a man of so few words."

"Yeah well, consider it a blessing."

Wyatt stepped towards me, inching ever so close. The only thing separating his body from mine was the car door. His eyes took me in, the disheveled mess I was, wild hair and morning breath included. I covered my mouth and stepped back.

"May I?" He inclined his head, holding out a hand for the blankets I used.

"Oh. Sure." *Derp*. I handed him the blankets and he bounced back to his folding spot, whistling a happy working tune.

"Are you always this chipper in the morning?"

He flashed me a dazzling smile. "Ya know, I slept really well. I haven't had a good night's sleep in forever. Maybe since I moved to New York."

He went back to his folding, resuming his whistle song. I blinked the sleep from my eyes and twisted my neck around.

"You must have the most uncomfortable bed in the world if the backseat of a car is an improvement."

"It's the noise. I just never got used to it."

He finished his folding and skipped along to the trunk to put them away. I went to the office where we'd left our bags, fished out my toothbrush and braved the scary bathroom, keeping the door cracked just a hair. Getting trapped in this bathroom was not the way I'd like to start my morning.

A short while later the mechanic arrived bearing two steamy coffee cups and a paper lunch bag. He had a rueful expression.

"My wife chewed me out last night."

"Oh no," I said. "Did you miss the pageant?"

"Oh, I got to the pageant on time. But later last night I told her about you guys staying here in the garage and she about flipped."

Wyatt shoved his hands in his jeans. "Sorry, man. We didn't mean to intrude—"

"She was so darn ticked off I didn't invite you to stay at our house. I can't figure her out. She practically carved me a new one the last time I had people over. I vowed never again. Then she pulls this guilt trip on me."

"Well, she'll be glad to learn Wyatt here slept like a baby, so no harm done."

He pressed his lips together and nodded with a sense of relief. "I'll let her know you said that." He blew out a sigh. "Whew. Pregnancy hormones."

Wyatt brightened at that. "Wow, another baby? I...I mean I saw the picture on your desk."

"Yup. Number four and counting."

"Awesome. I'm the oldest of six."

The mechanic's brows shot to his hairline. "Ya don't say."

Wyatt nodded proudly.

"Anyway," the mechanic gave the paper bag and coffee cups to Wyatt. "My wife made you her famous breakfast burritos. Her secret is the kielbasa sausages."

That sounded divine but I was definitely going on a pork fast after today.

"Thanks Claudio." I gave him a little hug and went off to zip my new moccasins in my suitcase. I'd left a couple of Benjamins and a note in the trunk of the Mustang, making sure Wyatt packed his moccasins, too.

After we said goodbye at the bus station, Wyatt shook his head at me. "What gave you the idea his name was Claudio? Or even Franz for that matter?"

"Just a guess. I didn't want to be rude and call him *Hey You*."

"I told you it's Al. His name patch, the sign on the auto shop, even the side of his truck says Al."

I blinked at him. "I thought that was the name of the town."

"Al, Nebraska? Really?"

A moment passed where I bat my eyes at Wyatt innocently and he gave me the *I don't buy it* glare.

"Okay," I caved. "The truth is, I'm terrible with names. So I make stuff up."

"Seriously? Al has to be the easiest name in the world. There's only two letters."

"Yeah, well." I shrugged. Surely I wasn't the only one who did that. Wasn't that normal? "I like to use first names of famous composers. Franz Liszt, Claudio Monteverdi, etcetera. It's usually only in my head, though."

The corner of Wyatt's mouth curled up.

"So what name did you give me?" he asked, eyes twinkling. It was the gold flecks catching the sunlight, probably.

"Wolfgang."

He nodded, letting that thought bounce around a bit. "Okay. I'm gonna go get the bus tickets. What was the town we need to go to?"

"Avery?"

"Right. Avery. You remember *that*."

I smiled proudly. "Oswald Theodore Avery. He's a founding father. Of *course* I remember that."

"Yeeeaaah. I'll be right back."

He took off, leaving Reeses with me, and returned a few minutes later, still laughing under his breath. "Wolfgang. Funny."

If you say so, buddy.

"I'm not gonna call you Wolfie if that's what you're thinking. Wyatt is much more interesting."

He gave me the side-eye. "Not sure if that's a compliment, but thanks."

He sipped the last of his coffee and winked. There was something refreshing about him. Perhaps it was his casual charm or the way his flyaway hair caught the sunlight, framing his face with an angelic glow. He was raggedy but confident in his own unique way. And that dimple. *Oof.*

A cloud of smoke billowed onto the bus platform. Down the way, an old monstrosity of a bus squeaked to a stop with a booming hiss, belching diesel exhaust. Large patches of rust covered most of the roof, corroding its way along the sides where the faded paint once displayed a patriotic red white and blue wave. Passengers piled on through both doors, carrying all sorts of parcels and bags. They certainly weren't wasting any time.

"Surely that's not our bus."

Wyatt smirked at me. "How much do you wanna bet?"

The driver came around the front and manually changed the destination sign to Avery.

"Oh, you gotta be kidding."

Wyatt tossed his coffee cup in the trash and laughed. "Come on before all the good seats are taken."

By the time we filed in behind half the population of Nebraska and all their cousins, Wyatt and I couldn't sit together. It shouldn't have made a difference to me but it did for some unexplainable reason. The lady occupying the seat next to me held a chicken on her lap. Wyatt had Reeses in that mesh travel bag and had to stand near the back. He had all his bags and the dog and held on tight to the metal bar while the bus lurched forward. I tried to take Reeses at one point but the chicken wasn't having it, batting its feathers, clucking like a maniac. It was inside a cage, but seemed to smell my fear, those beady eyes staring me down.

Yes, as a matter of fact I did have eggs for breakfast, Chickaletta.

The bus rambled along the highway, clattering with a thunderous roar. One of the windows not too far from me was stuck open, poorly remedied by a square of cardboard and some duct tape. The cold air still seeped through. Among the cornucopia of smells, even rising above the lovely aromatic sulfur of the diesel engine, was the arresting odor of farm animal. Probably goat. I didn't see any goats, nor did I hear the bleats of a goat, but there was definitely a goat on the bus.

I looked over at Wyatt. He threw me a silly grin trying to keep his balance. Admittedly, this chicken bus had certain advantages over New York's transportation system. The absence of mysterious sticky pee smelling blotches for starters.

And really, things weren't so terribly bad. I had a belly full of kielbasa burrito, we were on our way to Avery, it was two days until Christmas, and there was still a chance I'd make it to California by midnight if I could only get to an airport.

An elderly man with a long wiry beard made his way down the aisle at a slow pace, checking tickets. He wore a red tartan trapper hat and had a flush of pink on the end of his nose. He reminded me of a skinny corn-fed and wrinkly Santa Claus. Thirty-five minutes in and he was just now taking tickets. I wondered what he would do if there were any drifters on board. Halt the bus and throw them in the snow?

He approached, took the ticket from Chicken Lady and

made a little rip before handing it back. Then he held out his hand to me without even making eye contact.

I pointed back at Wyatt. "My friend has my ticket."

He frowned and moved on. So he was a skinny, wrinkly, *not jolly* Santa Claus. Ho ho ho.

Several minutes later, Wyatt's voice reached my ears. His tone was heightened and agitated. I turned to see Unjolly Santa shaking his head while Wyatt waved his arms around. I couldn't make out what he was saying, but it didn't appear seemly. The old man said something back, pointing out the window.

Oh gosh. He was going to throw us out into the snow. Did Wyatt lose the tickets? Scenes from *Polar Express* flashed through my head. I pictured myself on the roof of the moving bus, flurries of snow catching in my hair, conversing with a ghostly hobo while drinking coffee from a sock.

Wyatt stumbled over to me biting his lip.

"What's going on? Did you lose the tickets?"

"No, I have the tickets." He pulled them from his pocket.

"What's the problem then?"

He crinkled his nose, knit his eyebrows together, and said with a forced smile, "Funny story."

10

GEORGIA

Reeses barked at the rusty old bus as it rumbled its way down the road, leaving us on the outskirts of a small town. At this point, nothing surprised me. Wyatt raked his fingers through his unruly locks before sliding his beanie hat back on.

"So...what do you wanna do for two hours?"

"Is slapping you an option?"

"I said I was sorry." He paced back and forth, cursing under his breath. Then he pointed at his cheek. "Okay. Right here. Hit me with your best shot."

He held that position while I pretended to take him up on it. I wasn't about to slap him, for crying out loud, but letting him sweat it out wasn't beyond me.

I lifted my hand and tapped him on the cheek. "I'll take a rain check on that."

His Adam's apple bobbed. "That's not very encouraging."

"How were you supposed to know the difference between a bus to Avery, Nebraska and Avery, Missouri? It was too confusing."

"Yeah," he rallied. "And if they'd checked our tickets when we boarded, we could have caught the right one."

Reeses barked in solidarity. I bent down to scratch his little head. "You didn't like that chicken bus, anyhow, did you Reeses?"

His tongue hung out. I took that as a no.

Wyatt squinted in the distance. There was nothing for miles in either direction. We weren't even standing at a bus stop. But we were assured a bus would come along in a couple of hours, and that this was a regular stop on the route. A cluster of buildings, which we guessed, was a rural community sat about a quarter of a mile away from the highway.

Wyatt pointed that way. "Let's see if there's a cafe or something."

"You're not seriously hungry after that huge burrito."

He shrugged. "I could eat."

Unbelievable.

So we schlepped our luggage into town and ended up at a place called Burgers and Pies. At least that's what the sign outside said. Wyatt had his camera out and clicked at everything he found interesting along the way. Although not what I'd call picturesque, the town did have a certain rustic appeal one can't find in the coastal cities.

"My battery's almost gone," Wyatt said as we entered the diner. "I'm just going to ask if I can plug in my camera somewhere."

"What about your phone?"

He slipped it out of his jeans pocket. "Nah, I'm good."

We found a booth big enough for our bags, including Reeses' carrier, which we snuck in under Wyatt's coat. The poor dog was probably hungry by now even though he got some of our kielbasa scraps earlier.

Wyatt ordered a tall stack of pancakes and a side of chicken for Reeses. I had a glass of orange juice. As Wyatt devoured his second breakfast, sneaking bits of chicken to Reeses, he chatted merrily about what he wanted to see in California. He'd never been. He had idyllic visions of palm trees and sunny beaches and had plans to visit the Walk of Fame and the Hollywood sign. I just listened while he went on about it, not wanting to burst his bubble. Los Angeles wasn't so exciting in real life. He talked with childlike wonder of his hope to randomly bump into famous actors in restaurants, and just rub elbows with Hollywood elite at coffee shops or something. I tried to hold back a laugh at that.

"What?" he said. "Are you telling me you've never met a celebrity in all your years of living in LA?"

Had I met a celebrity? Hilarious.

"I didn't say anything."

"But you laughed." He took a big gulp of his water.

"I just don't think Julia Roberts gets her lattes at the corner Starbucks, that's all."

Wyatt sat back and dabbed his mouth with a napkin. "I'm sure there are hot spots. Actors are people just like you and me. They don't live like recluses. They go out."

I smiled, thinking of that interesting restaurant where my future sister-in-law used to work. Lucas Lodge. How my brother would frequent that place just to be close to her. How she'd bring him the type of beer he specifically didn't like just to mess with him.

How they fell in love without even realizing it.

I sighed with joy. "I suppose they do have to go out sometime."

Wyatt fed some more chicken to Reeses before returning to his pancakes.

"You know what this needs?" He dipped into his backpack and came up with a jar of gooseberry jam from the auto shop.

"Oh my gosh, Wyatt. Did you sneak that in your bag?"

"No. Al gave it to us, remember?" He smeared a generous glob on his pancakes and took a bite. "Mmmm. Oh wow. You gotta try this."

I swished a bit onto my finger and tasted the jam, licking the residue from my bottom lip. "Yummy."

Wyatt focused on my mouth for a long moment, a drop of jam dangling from his own.

"You've got a little..." I pointed at my mouth.

"Oh, thanks." He ran a napkin over his lips, and dug back into his meal trying to hide the soft blush blooming across his cheeks.

After a minute he cleared his throat. "So, if you could have lunch with any celebrity, who would it be?"

What a weird question. I shook my head. "Nobody."

"Oh come on. Who's your celebrity crush?"

"I don't have one."

He chuckled. "Sure you do. How about Chris Pine?"

I spurted a half-laugh. "Ewww. He's like a brother to me."

"What's that supposed to mean?"

"Uh," I sputtered. "I mean, he *seems* like the type of guy who'd be like, ya know, like a family friend. Like the friend of your brother or something. I don't know."

"I guess I can see what you mean. Natalie Portman is super pretty and all but she kinda looks like my sister. So crushing on her would be really gross."

"Yeah. Like that." I nodded.

"Emma Woods, on the other hand..." He whistled to complete his thought. "I don't have a sister that looks like *that*!"

Alrighty then. I won't be bringing that up to Emma when I see her at my brother's wedding.

Wyatt wagged his brows. "So now that I've made my confession, it's your turn. Every girl I know has the hots for *some* movie star or singer."

"I'm not every girl."

His breath hitched, the rise and fall of his chest more pronounced as he gazed at me in wonder. "No, you are not."

That boyish charm, I tell ya.

I cast my focus down, thumbing the plastic edge of the menu, thinking maybe I'd go for one of those pies after all—just to have something to do besides obsessing over this guy I just met. I couldn't bring myself to look back up at him. That dimple had a way of shooting right into my fluttery little heart. What was wrong with me? I learned my lesson with cute guys a while ago. Ya can't choose a book by his cover. Or something like that.

I'd known Jorge Wickham for years and still couldn't read between his devilish lines. He took advantage of my trust. How could I possibly think I knew anything about Dog Man?

"Georgia." Wyatt's voice was shaky. Tentative. I still didn't look up. "I...um." He faltered and I saw him scratch his day-old stubble in my peripheral vision. I'd noticed his scruff earlier and his little habit of running his hand over it. It kinda made my body react in a delightfully weird way.

"It's been a crazy twenty-four hours, huh?"

"Yeah." I looked up then, fixing my gaze on the sheen of his whiskers.

"Feels like we've known each other for a lot longer, though. Right?"

"Lots has happened," I agreed, ripping off a piece of his pancake. That really was delicious jam.

"So true." The slightest hint of a grin tugged at the corners of his mouth. "But despite the circumstances, I've enjoyed getting to know you."

"Me too."

His whole face brightened and his grin widened, those

dazzlingly white teeth almost blinding. "When we get to LA, do you think...maybe..."

He was cut off by the loud ping of his phone. He had it on the table next to his plate and it lit up with a text message.

"Is that my brother?"

He swept up the phone and typed a quick reply under the table before tossing it on the seat.

"Uh, no. Just my contact in LA."

"Oh. Is it about your 'top secret' news story?" I teased him with air quotes.

"Yeah." His expression darkened with just a flash, then he cleared his throat and took a sip of water.

"What were you saying before? About when we get to LA?"

He bit his bottom lip; chewing on whatever words he was about to say. For the first time, he looked right into my soul and reached across the table, wrapping his fingers around my hand. Shivers bolted up my arm and sped to my chest. I felt all glowy.

Then, two deafening blows cracked in my ears, shaking right through me. Wyatt felt it too because he cringed at the sound and scrunched his shoulders.

"What the—"

This was followed by some screams and movement at the other side of the restaurant. A strung-up looking guy climbed on top of a table with a gun in his hand. Another guy had a gun on the restaurant manager.

"This is a robbery." Table robber guy waved his gun around. People gasped and ducked. "Hands up where I can see them."

Some of the diner patrons were too shocked to respond, so he repeated himself, screaming at the top of his lungs. "I SAID, HANDS UP."

I immediately shot my arms in the air. Wyatt tossed his head around. Both robbers were out of earshot so he whispered. "Psst. Your ring."

"What?" I whispered back.

"Take your ring off."

"Why? It's fake."

"They don't know that. You want your finger cut off?"

Somehow I doubted the robbers would produce a machete out of their back pockets, but I took the ring off anyway, just in case. I slipped it in the seat cushions. Shostakovich's piano concerto no 2 would be a little tricky to play with a missing ring finger.

Most of the victims were silent. One lady was sobbing. The robbers barked some orders for the kitchen staff to come out and lie on the floor. They wanted anyone not in a booth to lie on the floor. Classic robbery protocol.

"Wallets and purses out, people. Put them on the table and no one gets hurt." The guy on the table jumped down, swiping up everything in sight.

The other guy had the manager empty the cash register. "Hurry up, old man."

Wyatt shifted in his seat, like he was winding up to do something heroic. I flashed him a warning look.

Don't even think about it.

He leaned over to tuck Reeses' carrier under the table, and in the process, his cell phone slipped off the seat onto the floor with a clank.

"What's going on over there?" The table guy came over. "You hidin' somethin'"?

He pointed the gun at Wyatt. Wyatt didn't flinch. Was he used to guns in his face or was he just stupid? I thought I might hyperventilate.

"Where's your wallet, tough guy?" The veins in the robber's neck bulged out.

"In my back pocket." Wyatt was cool. Samuel L. Jackson cool. But really not cool at all, if that makes sense.

"Well, hand it over."

Oh my gosh. Today was not a good day to die. My brother would kill me all over again.

Wyatt half-laughed. "Seriously? A scene out of *Pulp Fiction*? Not very creative of you."

"Who cares about creativity at a time like this?" I cried. "Give him your wallet."

"Listen to your lady, dimwit."

"Don't call me a dimwit," Wyatt said through clenched teeth.

"For goodness sakes, Wyatt. Give it to him. It's just money."

He flashed me a hard stare. "Says you."

Whoa.

Table robber didn't know what to do. The other guy was screaming at him to just shoot already. A dining patron cried out to Wyatt not to be an idiot. Actually, idiot wasn't the word he used. The sobbing lady was wailing for mercy. Reeses barked from under the table.

"Is that a dog? You got a dog under there?" The guy ducked to look, still pointing his gun at Wyatt. Reeses growled.

Wyatt glared coldly. "Yeah. Don't make me put him in kill mode."

Oh my heavens. We were dead for sure.

The robber laughed. His friend laughed. I wanted to disappear. Plus, my arms were getting tired.

In a flash, the robber fisted Wyatt's shirt, pulled him from the booth, punching him right on the jaw. The other guy cursed and shouted they should hurry up and get out. The sobbing lady screamed. Everyone else gasped. Chaos ensued.

And Wyatt blacked out.

11

WYATT

They took everything. Our luggage, my phone, my wallet. Everything except Reeses, and Georgia's fake diamond ring. I came to with a bag of ice on my face. The first thing I saw was Georgia's pointed scowl. A few other people stood over me to make sure I wasn't dead. Perhaps dissatisfied I wasn't, they walked off, shaking their heads.

Georgia frowned and crossed her arms. "Oh good. Now I can tell you off."

I rubbed my tender jaw. This should be fun.

"Reeses. Where's Reeses?"

"He's in the kitchen getting spoiled."

I peeled myself off the floor and sat on the edge of the booth. "Did the thieves get away?"

She waved her arms at the carnage of overturned tables and chairs. The gumball machine was a pile of broken glass and scattered gumballs on the floor. The pastry display was a sad, squishy mess.

"If you mean did the robbers get so angry because of you they wrecked the place and took all our stuff? Then yeah."

"Because of *me*? You're not blaming this on me."

She moved her hands to her hips. The Wonder Woman pose. My sisters used it on me. Worked every time. "What is wrong with you? Do you have a death wish?"

"No."

"Then why? *Whyyyy* did you insult the guy who was aiming a gun at your face?"

"Because he was ridiculous."

Her jaw hung open as she attempted to form words. Instead, grunts came out of her throat that sounded something like *Kuh*. It was still adorable coming from her. *Dangit*.

"It wasn't a real gun."

"Oh? And how do you know that?" she stuttered. "Are you a gun expert?"

"I know a paintball gun when I see one."

It took a moment for understanding to dawn on her face. She blinked a few times then came back with, "You still could have gotten hurt. It was pointed at your head."

"I was willing to take my chances."

"For a few bucks?" she cried. "Those guys were dangerous. They could have bludgeoned you."

"But they didn't."

"Says the guy who got knocked out in one punch."

"It was a fierce uppercut." I moved my jaw around. No missing teeth as far as I could tell.

"You are impossible. Seriously, I can barely tolerate you right now. In fact, I wish I'd never laid eyes on you. I *envy* people who haven't met you."

Her words punched a hole in my gut. It was more painful than the fist to my jaw.

"I couldn't let those simpletons take our luggage. Our traveling money."

"Who's the simpleton? You are. You're worse than a simpleton. You're a moron. I don't care about the stuff. It's nothing. It's not worth what you did."

"That's easy for a poor little rich girl to say. Why don't you call your daddy and ask for more money?"

That stopped her right there. But the shadow that fell over her face and the sleazy feeling on my skin made me wish I could take it back immediately. Dimples formed on her chin. Her nostrils flared. Her fists formed into tight balls, knuckles white with fury.

An apology was on the tip of my tongue but something stopped me from speaking. Perhaps it was the sting of her insults.

She took a steadying breath and lifted her chin, looking down on me with such disdain, I was certain I'd turned into slime on toast. With a swift sweep of her hand, she plucked up the gooseberry jam and stormed off.

I slunk in the booth, burying my face in my hands. That's when I noticed my empty plate.

"Those blockheads ate my pancakes."

I shrugged on my coat and went to check on Reeses. He was where Georgia said he was—in the kitchen. The cooks had given him a plate of ribs. He was so happy he didn't even acknowledge me when I walked in. The cooks served me up some dirty stares, though. At least they didn't kick me out.

One of them nodded towards the rear exit with a pointed look. I followed his gaze and pushed through the flimsy door. There was Georgia outside in the freezing air, sitting on a milk crate. Fuming. She was so hot with rage; the atmosphere around her was its own weather system. But her eyes, when they landed on me were cold as ice.

"Do you want to cash in on that face slap?" I said with a sorry attempt at humor.

"Go away."

"You're right. I *am* a moron."

She half-laughed, not in a good way.

I went on. "Some people just need a high five. In the face. With a chair."

That at least earned me an eye roll.

"I'm a simpleton. I'm the mayor of Simpleton. And I'm sorry."

She wasn't ready to speak. There was still a lot of anger in the air. But she breathed a heavy sigh, staring at the ground thoughtfully. Most likely agreeing with me.

I found another milk crate and set myself down next to her. It was confession time. Ever since I'd moved to New York I painted myself up as a clown. It was a facade mostly to fool myself. A way to bury the ever-present stress of a starving artist. A way to avoid the disheartening fear of failure. That maybe if I ignored the rejections, I might be able to make it one day. And make my parents proud.

My thoughts turned to the gig in LA. I knew it was a risk—packing all my worldly possessions in a suitcase to chase a Hollywood gossip story. That's not what I was about. I had dreams of selling a spec script. Not selling my soul to a click farm. But my friend assured me the whole thing was super low profile. No press. And I was desperate for the cash.

I laced my fingers together and rested my elbows on my knees. Contrite as could be. "It was stupid of me to stand up to the robbers like that."

"Ya think?"

Sharp. Sarcastic. Biting. I'd take that over the silent treatment.

"That was everything I owned. The stuff they took. It's funny how feral you can get when you've got nothing left to lose."

She turned her head to me a tiny bit. "What do you mean, everything you owned?"

I flipped up my palms. "It's just how it sounds. My roommate got a cat. Hated dogs. His apartment. His rules. My loss. So I packed up, emptied my bank account, and got on a plane." I made an airplane gesture with my hand to illustrate.

Georgia considered my words for a moment before saying, "You mean those bags...that was all your stuff in the world?"

I nodded. "I mean, I left some things behind at my parent's house. A beat-up guitar I play poorly. My old baseball cards. A bowling ball."

She was silent for some time, I supposed trying to wrap her brain around my plight. My circumstances must have sounded extreme. So far removed from her world. But I wasn't trying to be dramatic. I just wanted her to understand.

"So that's why I put up a fight. I didn't think about you or anyone else in that diner. So I'm sorry. Also the robbers ate my pancakes, so..."

A smile cracked on her features. "And you go crazy when you're hungry?"

"Something like that."

She cast her eyes down, passing the jar of gooseberry jam back and forth between her hands.

"I'm sorry I called you a moron."

"Nope. I deserved that. I'm sorry I insulted your...richness." I sighed, pinching the bridge of my nose. "See, I liked a girl in college who came from money. A daddy's girl. But she was pure evil. I guess those old feelings came flooding back. It's no excuse but I'm sorry just the same."

"What makes you think I'm rich?"

I ticked my fingers. "College student. First class seat. American Express black card. Loads of cash. It's a wild guess."

"Graduate student. And I'm not a daddy's girl." She ran her

thumb across the label on the jam jar with a hint of lonesome recollection. "I'm an orphan."

Then she quickly added, "Orphan, someone who has lost their parents. Not often frequently."

I blinked at her. "You know that joke only works with an English accent."

And just like that, she cracked up. My heart felt a thousand pounds lighter and for that tiny suspended moment in time, the world felt right. Everything was going to work out just fine.

Until the manager poked his head outside to announce the police had arrived. Then everything shifted.

We went inside and waited our turn to make a statement. I heard one of the officers flippantly declare, "This sort of thing happens in these parts every year at Christmas time."

Every. Year.

One would think somebody would get wise after all this time and hire a security guard. But the officers took statement after statement with bored expressions.

Then they got to me. Wrote down my full name. Wyatt Boyd Silva. The cops chuckled when the restaurant manager told them of my stupidity. So I informed them the robbers had paintball guns and grinned with a healthy dose of satisfaction.

Boo-yah.

Then they moved on to Georgia. Wrote down her full name. And my heart sank.

Georgia Marie Darcy.

Darcy. It wasn't a common surname. It was akin to the likes of Presley or Disney or Barrymore. It was an elite name. A famous name.

I tried to reason with my clouded brain that maybe her name was more common than I'd thought. But the clues were there all along. And when the officers grilled her about it, my suspicions were confirmed.

"Yes," she said with trepidation. "He's my brother. Please don't leak this to the press."

She uttered the word 'press' with definitive ire, like it was poison on her lips. She hated the press.

But I was the press. A slime ball in her eyes. The guy with the inside scoop on the biggest secret in Hollywood. Will Darcy's hush-hush wedding.

My exclusive story.

My throat swelled. My palms clammed up. I was feverish all over with dread.

Just my luck.

The girl I started to have feelings for was Will Darcy's little sister.

12

GEORGIA

Wyatt was uncharacteristically quiet as we finally left the restaurant. Sure, he'd just been robbed of virtually everything he owned, but a tiny bit of luck did shine down upon him, so I figured he'd be a little more chipper. Turned out, in all the hullabaloo, and in an effort to get outta there before the cops showed up, the robbers overlooked Wyatt's camera, which was tucked under a counter, plugged into the power socket. Hooray for small miracles.

We made our way back to the highway much later than we'd originally planned. Reeses trotted along at our feet wagging his tail, happy as a clam. Completely oblivious. To him it was just another day in the life of the most adorable Jack Russell terrier in the world.

"I guess we missed the bus," I said.

Wyatt continued in silence.

"Do you suppose another one will come along?"

He only responded with a grunt. I hadn't bothered to ask anyone about busses back in the diner—seeing as how they all wished they could slip arsenic in our to-go cups. The only reason we got free sodas to go was because they were handing them out to everybody. We weren't special. In fact, everyone just wanted us to leave already.

We reached the spot where the bus had dropped us off earlier. I didn't have a watch, but I was pretty sure two hours had passed quite a while ago. The sun was low in the sky and the afternoon winter chill descended upon us with a blanket of gloom. That bus was long gone.

Neither one of us spoke for some time, standing there on the side of the road feeling stupid. I said a silent prayer hoping things would turn around for us. At this point, I'd happily go back to spend another night in that vintage Mustang. Anywhere but here.

Wyatt's silent treatment wasn't directed at me. He didn't seem angry. Just...retrospective. We'd had a moment in the back alley of the restaurant. A heart to heart if you will. It took a lot of courage for him to admit to a stranger those things he said to me. Then again, we didn't feel like strangers anymore. I thought we'd crossed some proverbial bridge. There was a connection there. He was as jolly as a North Pole elf. But when the police officers were taking our statements, I caught the moment when a shadow crossed Wyatt's features. It was when the officer discovered who my famous brother was. I turned to find Wyatt's eyes locked on me, glum and crestfallen by my lie of omission.

His face reminded me of those mimes in Manhattan who swipe smiles into frowns with a wave of a hand. I wanted to wave my hand in front Wyatt's face to turn that frown upside down.

In my defense, the subject of last names never came up in the strange circumstances we found ourselves in. At least that's what I told myself. In truth, I was tired of users. People who pretended to be my friend but only wanted to get at my famous brother.

Besides. What was I supposed to say to Wyatt while we

were thrust in this weird situation anyway? *Oh by the way, my brother is a movie star. Moving on.*

As I watched Wyatt retreat farther into his thoughts, I told myself there must be some other explanation. Maybe he was trying hard not to burp or something.

He kicked his shoe against the edge of the asphalt, soooo enthralled by the uneven pavement.

Ah! Bumpy. So cool.

The highway went on for miles in each direction with nothing in sight. Just lots of flat flatness. And snow.

Then something caught my eye. About a hundred feet away, the road was littered with debris. Things I couldn't quite make out were scattered here and there. *Somebody* was a litterbug. I tilted my head and took a few steps.

"Wait a minute." I took a few more steps. "Wyatt, check this out."

He came over followed by Reeses and before we knew it we were sprinting towards the debris. Except as we got closer, we discovered that stuff was more than just trash. There were empty wallets and purses, a ripped up denim jacket, a discarded cigarette package, a lipstick, and lots of miscellaneous wrappers and papers.

"As if robbery wasn't enough, let's make it interesting by trashing the highway," I deadpanned.

Wyatt went around picking up the items with his one hand. I joined in to help him.

"You wanna bring this stuff back?" I suggested, even though I didn't want to.

"No. Let's just consolidate it and pile it on the side of the road out of the way of passing cars."

"Good idea," I agreed.

It took longer to pick stuff up one-handed, but neither one

of us wanted to set down our sodas for some reason. Then I found a phone. Cracked screen, scuffs all over.

"Is this yours?" I held it up for Wyatt to see.

His face lit up. "Yeah."

"Maybe your luck is turning around," I said.

"Doubtful." He turned it over in his hand. "It's even more cracked than before. And the case is missing."

"Does it work?"

He tapped it, raising his brows. "Actually, yeah."

"Maybe we can find your wallet," I said, hopeful.

"And your purse."

I shook my head. "Everything was inside my carry-on. I'd have found it by now."

We kept on down the road, picking up stuff as we got farther and farther away from the turnoff to the little town. It occurred to me we'd get to California faster by walking if we'd have just avoided all the modes of transportation we'd attempted.

We reached what appeared to be the end of the items discarded out of the robber's window. Wyatt's wallet wasn't on the road. We'd just made the last pile of stuff when a rickety black truck came down the highway, slowing down when we were in sight and stopping right by us. There was a cobra painted on the hood.

A middle-aged man rolled down the window, taking in the sight of all the litter. He had wild eyes. It was a little scary. "What's goin' on here?" His voice was more of a growl.

I spoke up. "Just cleaning the highway."

He squinted, thick salt-and-pepper brows furrowed over his eyes. "Why?"

"We care about the environment?"

Then Wyatt stepped in front of me, a small gesture, but a protective one just the same. "We were robbed and hoping to find some of our things."

The man nodded thoughtfully, glancing back at the turnoff to the tiny town. "At the pie place back there?"

"Yes," Wyatt and I said in unison.

"Sounds about right. Happens every year."

So we'd been told.

"Listen," I said, hoping for answers. This guy had a seriously ominous vibe going on but he seemed to know what was up around these parts. "Do you know if there are any more busses scheduled to come by? We missed our bus while we were filing the police report."

The man studied us for a long moment, rolled down the driver's side window, spat, then turned back to us. "Which way you headed?"

"We were headed to Avery, Missouri," Wyatt said. "But we're on our way to California."

The man grunted. "You're a ways off from Missouri. And it's the wrong direction if you want to get to California."

Yeah, we get that.

"There ain't no more busses far as I know."

Disappointment shot through me. We were penniless and stuck in the middle of nowhere. And I resolutely drew the line at hitchhiking.

"I can take you as far as I can," said the man.

I was poised to decline when Wyatt asked, "Where are you headed?"

"South."

Oh great. Not vague at all.

Wyatt turned to me, eyes bright, all hopeful and cheery. Old Wyatt was back. His expression declared, *We've been saved!*

I hoped my face communicated my alarm. *No! Run away. Stranger danger.*

He took me aside. "We don't have to go back to Avery. We can keep going South."

"I'm not getting in a truck with Wild-Eyes Ludwig."

"What's the alternative? Walk to California?"

How did he know the thought had crossed my mind? "Maybe the cops can take us somewhere safe."

Wyatt snorted. "Those guys? Fat chance."

He had a point. Officer 1 and officer 2 were a couple of good 'ol boys. Right before we took off I noticed them raiding the beer fridge.

"Ya comin' or not?" The guy was growing impatient but Wyatt held my shoulders at arm's length, leveling his eyes to mine. "Alright. We'll wait for the bus."

There was no bus. And even if there was one, we weren't guaranteed they'd honor our tickets. Wyatt clapped his hand on the passenger side window frame and offered a grateful smile at the man. "Thanks, but we're gonna stick around here for a while."

"Suit yourselves." The man put the truck in gear.

"Wait." I ran to stop him. "We accept."

He gave me a stern look. "You *ax-cept?*" He said the word like it tasted bad on his tongue.

"Yes. We accept your offer to give us a ride."

He shook his head. His expression was all, *'weird out-of-towners'* and he set the gear back to park. We shuffled in, Wyatt taking the center seat. Reeses on my lap.

The ride was uncomfortable in more ways than one. The interior of the truck smelled of tobacco and something musty. Every now and then the man would hawk a loogie out the window, and Wyatt's many attempts at conversation were abruptly cut off. Wyatt introduced himself, me and Reeses, but was met with silence. The man had absolutely no interest in chatter nor did he find it necessary to tell us his name.

We rode as the sun began to set. The thought at the forefront of my mind the entire time being: *Where exactly South are we going?*

Studying his profile, I noticed the deep-set lines on the man's face. The heavy, loose skin under his eyes making him appear more like a basset hound. The permanent scowl on his features. He had a faint scar on his chin. And his left hand had two missing fingers.

About an hour in, he pulled onto a dirt road. The soft slush of snow mixed with the earth to form muddy ice trails in lieu of tire tracks. The surroundings became increasingly overgrown with evergreens and wild brush as we progressed to this mysterious—and alarmingly remote—destination. The man didn't say a word until he parked in front of a decrepit shack. A felled tree stretched the front of the property, serving no purpose other than to make the place appear abandoned. Old tires were strewn haphazardly in random spots, and the disturbing presence of an ax perched prominently on a chopping block right in front of the truck.

"I'll just be a minute." With a grunt, the man lowered himself from the truck and slammed the door shut. Wyatt's Adam's apple bobbed. We exchanged a frightened look.

The man rounded to the back of the truck, opened the tailgate, and slid out something heavy inside a large, black bag. He slumped it over his shoulder and disappeared around the back of the shack.

"Wyatt?"

"Yeah?"

"What do you think is in that bag?"

He swallowed hard. "I'm afraid to find out."

"Was that my imagination, or did that look like a body?"

He didn't answer. He was thinking what I was thinking. This was the sort of place people went missing.

"Wyatt?"

"Shhh."

"I have to pee." I shouldn't have polished off that soda.

"Hold it."

A minute or two later, the man returned. He got in the truck without a word, his expressionless face betraying nothing, and he drove us back onto the main highway. The air was thick. Any minute now we could be dead meat. Was this how he lured his victims? Where was he taking us? If I survived this, there was *no way* I'd tell my brother.

We crossed the Kansas state line a while later and before we knew it, the twinkly lights of a quaint little town came into view. As we entered the center of town, the sight was an explosion of Christmas. Garlands hung from every surface creating a canopy of green over the streets from the rooftops to the lampposts. All the shops were decked out with wreaths and bright red bows. Colored lights covered every tree. Was that a gazebo in the town square? I could have sworn we'd stumbled upon a Hallmark movie sound stage.

"This is as far as I go." The scary man pulled over to the curb, the truck still running. In other words, "*Get out.*"

So, you're not going to kill us after all?

Wyatt breathed a sigh of relief. "I can't thank you enough for the ride."

The man responded with a minuscule nod.

"Where are we, anyway?"

Stop asking questions, genius. Let's go.

But something in the man's features softened for one fleeting moment when he said, "Bethlehem."

Wyatt ruined the moment with a snort. "You're joking, right?"

He was met with a cold stare. "Do I look like I joke?"

"No, sir."

My bladder couldn't take it anymore. I had to find a bathroom.

"Thanks again," I said, opening my door. "Is there anything we can do to repay you?"

He turned his scowly face and for the first time since he picked us up, really looked at me and Wyatt. He opened his mouth to speak, pausing as though words were just too much trouble and not really worth the effort. But then he focused on Wyatt, surprising us with this gem:

"Tell your woman you love her every day. Promise me that?"

Wyatt nodded. "Yes, sir. I promise."

The man cast his eyes on me, and then back to Wyatt, then down to where Wyatt unintentionally rested his hand on my knee and said, "Never take each other for granted. Cherish every moment because life is short."

Then he shooed us out of the truck and we wished him a Merry Christmas as he drove away.

We stood on the sidewalk all aglow from the warm string lights overhead and laughed. Grateful to be alive. Amazed, elated, and perplexed. And happy. It was strange but I couldn't think of anyone else I'd rather share this with. It was uniquely ours.

Wyatt scanned our surroundings. "So. Little town of Bethlehem. Let's see if we have to sleep in a stable."

13

GEORGIA

It could have been an idyllic scene. A soft flurry of snow cascading onto the red stone-paved street, colonial brick buildings with brightly-lit shop windows and welcoming entryways, old fashioned street lamps, and—did I hear Christmas music piped onto the sidewalks? I wouldn't be surprised if the buttery aroma of popcorn reached my nose through hidden vents. There I was, strolling along Main Street, Bethlehem with a sweet dog and even sweeter man. It *could* have been idyllic—if we weren't completely lost.

"Did we just teleport into Disneyland?" I joked. "Now I want a churro."

Wyatt grinned. "Another place on my bucket list."

"It's so fun during the holidays," I said with a sigh. "Main Street looks just like this but not as cold. Then there's the giant turkey legs."

My stomach growled.

"I heard that."

I was too tired, grubby, and hungry to be embarrassed. "What do we do now?"

"First, you should report your credit cards stolen." He

handed me his battered phone. "Then call your brother...*'Billy'*. Or should I call him Will?"

"I'm sorry I didn't tell you before."

"You don't need to apologize. I haven't bored you with a list of names of all *my* siblings. It's no big deal."

"Really?" It was usually a big deal to most people I'd meet. It's not fun being the sister of Celeb Magazine's *Sexiest Man Alive*.

Wyatt cradled my chin, brushing his thumb along my cheek. "Really."

Gah!

Wyatt took Reeses to do his business while I called my brother. I was relieved it went to voicemail. I left a quick, chirpy message to please report my credit cards stolen, keeping it light.

I'm fine. Just got robbed. No big deal. Ha ha. Bye.

I wasn't looking forward to his reply. In fact, I didn't think Wyatt's battery would last that long. It was at ten percent. Why did the guy not plug it in when I'd suggested it?

I found him a few minutes later chatting it up with an old woman. She was the quintessential grandma. Warm smile, rosy cheeks, and a puff of white curls atop her head. Reeses was all over the attention, licking her face as she cradled him in her arms.

"I had Russell Terriers all my life," she said scratching Reeses behind the ears. "Jo Jo was such a spitfire. Always getting into things."

When she noticed me her eyes twinkled and she smiled sweetly. "Hello there. You must be the bride."

The bride?

Wyatt looked at me like *"Just go with it."* So I extended my hand in greeting. "I'm Georgia."

"Oh, we don't shake hands around here," she said, and pulled me into an awkward hug with Reeses between us.

I patted her back. "Oh, okay."

She handed Reeses over to Wyatt. "I look forward to seeing you two later."

With a wink and a final dog kiss, she strolled off.

"The bride?"

Wyatt shrugged. "She just kinda assumed."

"Anyway, we need to plug this in." I handed back his phone. "It's almost dead."

"Oh fiddlesticks."

Fiddlesticks? This guy.

He winced. "The charger was in my backpack."

"Oh. Fiddlesticks is right."

We were officially out of luck. No money, no identification, no phone. Also no change of clothes, no toothbrush, no transportation...the list was laughable.

He frowned at his phone. "Rats."

I shook my head at him and chuckled at all the absurdities of the last two days. He really was the unluckiest guy I'd ever met. "You should have named your dog Snoopy."

"Snoopy? Why's that?"

"Because you, my friend, are Charlie Brown."

A grin cracked across his beautiful face. "Does that make you the red-haired girl?"

My cheeks burned bright. I tried to cover them with my gloved hands. Changing the subject was also a good tactic.

"Moving on. Who was that lady?"

"Oh, just Reeses' newest friend. She told me all about her grandkids. I practically know her whole family now. How long were you gone?"

A couple minutes tops.

"She seemed...friendly."

"She was, in fact. Her grandson plays a shepherd boy in the local church's Living Nativity. His name is A.J., he's six years old, and he wants Spiderman underwear for Christmas. Oh, and he likes to cook. He wants to be a chef. Apparently he makes a fantastic banana bread."

"That's quite a lot of information."

He bobbed his head animatedly. "So, you want to go?"

"Go where?"

"To the Living Nativity. Remember that commercial we heard? This must be it."

"We were pretty far away from here when we heard that commercial. And that car radio didn't have a very good antenna."

"Maybe it's a Christmas miracle."

Oh, Wyatt and his Christmas miracles.

"It will be a Christmas miracle if they have food at this thing."

Wyatt set Reeses down and wrapped his arm around my shoulders. His gleeful smile shot right to the feels—his face just inches from mine as he squeezed me. He meant it as a friendly gesture but this close to him my nerves jumped to attention. There was warmth in his orbit. The scent that was all Wyatt crept into my senses and made me a little tipsy. I reeled on my feet.

"You alright?"

Not at all.

"Yeah. Just hungry, I guess."

With a look of concern, he released me to offer his arm. "I have it on good authority there'll be the best banana bread in the world and maybe some of Grandma's homemade fudge."

"Sounds fancy." I took his arm. It was so cute, because his chest puffed up with the task of escorting me to the church thing.

He winked and I was done. My belly about flipped over.

"Only the best for Miss Darcy."

14

WYATT

Note to self: When asking for directions in a small town, *"Just around the corner"* actually means *"Pass the courthouse, down the street, turn right at Lu Lu's Bakery, go around some stables, keep going down a back road outside of town, and another half-mile on the left."*

When we arrived at Hope Evangelical Christian Church, even though it wasn't any further than my usual commute in Manhattan, I was frozen to the bone from the walk. Those things inside my Converse All Stars? They weren't feet anymore. They were the most unpleasant popsicles in the universe.

Georgia, who'd planned her wardrobe better than me, was rosy-cheeked and fresh. She could have been on one of those York Peppermint Patty commercials. The cloud from her mouth when she breathed seemed to turn to crystal before floating away to frost nearby windowpanes. Or evergreen trees. Or perhaps turn into gleaming castles of ice with silvery spires jutting heavenward.

Clearly, I put too much thought into Georgia's minty breath.

I carried Reeses in his bag so his little paws wouldn't freeze. I'd given him my scarf. He was living the good life.

The church was an old converted barn, renovated to accommodate a fairly large congregation. It was enormous. There were different doors off the main sanctuary, most likely leading to meeting rooms, childcare, or offices. As we entered, a group of teens rushed past us, laden with robes of various colors, plaster wings, and glittery headpieces. A woman with a clipboard worked in the far corner wrangling small children and several others mulled around chatting or getting ready for the performance.

"I guess we're a little early," said Georgia, looking around.

"It would seem so. I'm just waiting for my feet to thaw out."

She *tsked* at me. "You don't own a pair of boots, do you?"

I admitted that I did not. I liked my converse.

A door swung open and a pretty woman in her forties rushed through wearing an apron. She had an air of authority about her—the way she carried herself maybe, or perhaps how heads turned as she entered the room.

"Has anyone seen Tom and Denise?" she called out.

Someone shouted back they had the flu. Or was it they had to glue? Could have been either. There was too much activity going on to hear well.

The woman in the apron slumped a little, pressing her temple before clapping eyes on us. She came over.

"Oh thank goodness. Are you two here to serve?"

She gave us each a hug. "I've never seen a turn out like this in all the years we've been running the soup kitchen. I think it's because word got out someone donated all that turkey."

Georgia instinctively clutched her coat in the area of her stomach. "Did you say turkey?"

"Isn't that wonderful? We are blessed beyond measure. But we're swamped in there. You...*did* come to volunteer, right?"

"Yes," Georgia blurted. "Absolutely. That's why we're here."

The woman pressed her heart and smiled sweetly. Then, as she ushered us to the kitchen, she introduced herself. "I'm Teresa, by the way. I'll get you set up."

She found a couple of aprons and handed them over. "I don't think I've seen you around before."

Georgia introduced us, including Reeses, and said we were just passing through. She didn't get into the crazy details. Teresa would hardly believe it anyway.

Before I knew what was happening, they were chatting like besties, giggling about how Georgia drowned in the large apron. How cute her earrings were. Exchanging make-up hacks.

I excused myself to set Reeses up with a bowl of water. I don't think the ladies noticed my absence. A pot-bellied man called me over and tossed a hairnet at me.

"You'll be on mashed potatoes."

He pointed a carving knife toward the buffet and hunched back over the turkey. I could tell he was serious about slicing. They don't give that job to just anybody.

I took my spot behind the serving line flanked by two elderly women. A box of latex gloves was passed along which both the ladies refused to use.

"I'm not afraid to get my hands dirty," one of them said as she tossed the box to the next guy. I was pretty sure the gloves weren't for her benefit but who was I to say?

I got to work dolloping spoonfuls of mashed potatoes while the granny next to me smothered them in gravy with a drippy splat. After a few minutes we'd developed a well-timed system.

Scoop, splat. Scoop, splat.

At one point we were in rhythm with the Christmas music. The lady on the other side of me was in her own world, singing and bopping out while on green bean duty.

Hordes of people came through the line. Teresa wasn't

kidding. But the community there for the free holiday dinner was different from the usual crowd I'd seen go into New York soup kitchens. These were families, farmers, working folk. And they were ever grateful.

I caught a glimpse of Georgia passing out dinner rolls with a generous portion of smiles. She was resplendent. A couple of teen boys held up the line because they didn't want to part from her.

Move it along, boys.

Scoop, splat. Scoop, splat.

In the end we went through eight trays of spuds. I heard somebody estimate about two hundred people came through. Even so, there was plenty left over for the volunteers. Who knows where all that food came from? It was like the loaves and fishes.

Later, when Georgia pushed her plate away and tugged to stretch her waistband I nudged her with my shoulder and gave her an *I told you so* look.

"I think we can safely say this qualifies as a Christmas miracle."

She just laughed.

Teresa joined us soon after with a plate of cookies to share apologizing because the good ones were the first to go. We couldn't eat another bite anyway. She thanked us for the seventy-ninth time.

"Believe me, the pleasure was all ours," I assured her.

She clasped her hands over ours. "Are you staying for the Living Nativity?"

"Wouldn't miss it," Georgia said, grinning adorably. "I hear A.J. hits it out of the park with his shepherd boy performance."

Teresa's eyebrows shot up. "You know A.J. Tucker?"

"Not exactly." Georgia explained how we'd met the grandmother in town and that's what brought us here.

"And the commercial," I added. "Don't forget about that."

Georgia cast her eyes to the ceiling. She still wasn't convinced the signal could have gotten that far.

"The commercial was my husband's idea," said Teresa.

I grinned at Georgia, mouthing the words *Christmas miracle*.

It was so satisfying.

"Oh, speaking of my husband, he's waving me over. Gotta go." Teresa gave Georgia a tight squeeze. "Hope you enjoy the walk-through. See you at the finish."

Georgia crinkled her nose as Teresa danced away. "Walk-through?"

15

WYATT

It was fun to tease Georgia about the Christmas miracle thing. But the real miracle was her. How she stumbled into my life and suddenly the world was beautiful again. Okay, Reeses had something to do with the stumbling part but I considered it a miracle just the same.

We lived in a city of millions. Perfect strangers with completely different lives. I could have passed her on 14th street and never had a reason to talk to her. Yet here we were in Bethlehem, Kansas. Falling in love.

Whoa there, Wyatt.

What did that dear old granny put in the gravy?

I knew I was falling in *something*. The woozy feeling in my stomach told me as much. But love? How would I know? I had nothing to compare it with.

We entered the sanctuary as people were taking their seats. A group of about a dozen ladies came in through the front door. They were all smiles, giggling amongst themselves. But there was something about them I couldn't quite put my finger on.

"I wonder who they are," said Georgia, following my line of sight. "They're all wearing the same thing. Like a uniform."

Ah, that's what it was. Each of them wore a long, beige skirt and the same white collars peeked out from under their winter coats. They had some sort of metal brooch in the shape of a heart pinned to cream cardigans, from what I could see when a coat or two was unzipped. And each and every one of them had short hairstyles. But the one thing that particularly stood out was the joy on their faces. Like they were all glowy from the inside out.

"Maybe they work at See's Candy," I suggested. "They're so happy."

Georgia chuckled. "I'd be happy, too, if I worked in a candy store."

We moved to look for our seats when A.J.'s grandma seemingly appeared out of nowhere.

"I'm so happy you decided to come." Hugs and wet kisses on the cheek were part of the greeting package with this woman. We soon found out what Teresa meant by walk-through. A.J.'s grandma explained the whole thing. Although the opening scene was to take place inside the main sanctuary, the rest of the reenactment was a walking tour outside guided by a little boy with a snare drum.

"Don't worry." said she. "Pastor Kevin put up space heaters along the route. And the actors have plenty of layers."

By *actors* she meant townsfolk and their children. It was a tradition at this church and apparently the congregants looked forward to this night all year long. They were kinda obsessed with it according to A.J.'s grandma.

The old woman leaned in to whisper, "I heard Suzy McCormick got pregnant again on purpose just so her kid could play Baby Jesus this year. She's no Virgin Mary, I'll tell you that much."

T.M.I. lady.

We sat down right before the lights dimmed. Our new

friend dropped off a plate of fudge at a refreshments table and swiftly returned to join us. She certainly loved to talk, chatting in Georgia's ear all throughout Pastor Kevin's intro speech. I think she was thrilled to have fresh ears who hadn't heard all her stories before. Georgia was bright enough to get her name. Lois. She looked like a Lois.

At one point she asked how we came to pass by Bethlehem of all places. Georgia told her how we hitched a ride with the man with the black truck, highlighting the detail about the snake on the hood.

"Oh that would be Walter," chirped Lois. "Such a nice man. Did he tell you about his daughter? Big time lawyer in the city. He's so proud."

That piqued my interest. "No he didn't. Not much of a talker."

According to Lois, Walter went to live with his daughter after his wife passed away. He'd made the trip back to Bethlehem every month to place fresh flowers on her grave and on Christmas, he and his daughter had the tradition to meet at his little cabin just over the state line.

Georgia and I exchanged a look. We were so off.

Pastor Kevin finished his intro and the congregation applauded as the stage lights turned to a blueish hue and music rose through the speakers. It was a lesser-known carol called Gabriel's Message beautifully performed by the children's choir. As they sang, a young lady dressed in a blue veil came on stage accompanied by a boy dressed as an angel.

"Is that Suzy McCormick?" asked Georgia in a whisper.

"Heavens, no," said Lois. "That's the pastor's daughter, Joy. She's only fifteen. You'll see Suzy later."

Oh yippee.

When the song ended, a scripture was read and we were instructed to follow the drummer boy outside. We all filed out.

Since we were towards the back, we ended up getting clumped in the straggler's section but that didn't dilute our experience.

It was a walking tour of the nativity story. Costumed characters stood in perfectly still vignettes like statues in a scene. Large scrolls served to indicate what scene we were passing. There was the angel appearing to Joseph in a dream. The teen boy playing Joseph did a good job at acting frightened.

There was Mary (played by yet another girl) visiting her cousin Elizabeth. We walked further down to see the Herod scene played out by a ten-year-old boy lying on a mountain of gold. That was a little disturbing.

Then another two actors playing Mary and Joseph traveling to Bethlehem on a Donkey. They had a real donkey.

I was about to be extremely impressed by that until I spotted the camels. Where the heck did they get three camels? These guys weren't fooling around with their nativity show.

"Watch out," said Lois, nudging us with her arm. "Those creatures like to spit."

Georgia chuckled. "I'll bear that in mind."

I clung tight onto Reeses just in case. His furry little ears perked to attention at the sight of all the other animals.

"Do you want to play with the camels, Reeses?" He responded to my question by licking my face.

Finally we reached a choir of angels singing *Gloria In Excelsis Deo* to a group of shepherds. Of course there were real sheep. Why not?

That's when Lois whipped out her camera, clicking away at a particular shepherd who exposed his toothless grin at his Grandma every time the flash went off. Georgia and I stayed behind with her as those in line behind us passed to the next station.

"That must be the incredible A.J. we've heard so much about," said Georgia as she waved at the boy. He waved back with unbridled enthusiasm. All the other shepherds were frozen in their poses. Not A.J.

"Hi Grandma! Hi." More energetic waves. "Hiiiiiiii."

He was quite a bouncy little kid.

Lois got out of line to give him hugs and passed him some candy canes.

We continued on. I was surprised the heat lamps worked so well. I didn't feel the cold. And then we came upon the main tableau.

They spared no detail with the crèche scene. It was as picturesque as a Michelangelo painting. A wooden structure to resemble a stable stood prominently on a raised stage, which was covered in hay to resemble a tiny hill. Shepherds and barn animals surrounded the Holy Family. Everyone posed perfectly still.

That didn't seem to sit right with Reeses who wiggled out of my arms and bolted to warn the other animals that their humans were comatose or maybe taxidermic. He leaped onto the scene, barking, issuing his battle call.

Beware fellow four-footed friends. It's PEOPLE!

He spooked the sheep and the horses. Grown men dressed as shepherds tried to calm the animals by double-downing on their tethers.

"Reeses, get back here." I chased him into the nativity scene, stepping over the empty manger to catch him. I don't know what got into him. He was usually better behaved than me.

He yelped at me as if to say *Run! Save yourself while you can. They're stuffing humans.*

So I dove for it. The sheep bleated. The horse neighed. The humans gasped.

But I got him, squirmy little bugger.

"What's got into you, peanut butter cup?"

That's when I noticed my foot was tangled in Mary's robes.

My shoe had somehow gotten caught on the hem, dragging the fabric with me as I flew through to catch my dog. There was a mile of fabric and I was stepping on a piece of it. The rest of the skirt rode up to her waist, exposing her long johns and almost covering the baby in her arms. He was fast asleep, not bothered by any of it thank goodness.

"Sorry ma'am." I righted her skirt, fluffing it up into a giant, pillowy meringue.

Joseph scowled at me.

I scooped up Reeses and returned to Georgia. She covered her face, likely embarrassed to be seen with me, but Lois laughed like it was the best thing she'd seen all year.

"*That* is Suzy McCormick," she said, doubling over. "And now you've been aquatinted."

"Lucky me." I sent Reeses back into his bag. "You're in trouble, mister."

Lois was watching Suzy, shaking her head. "She insisted on making her own costume."

"Well, that's pretty crafty of her," said Georgia. "I can't sew to save my life."

Suzy was the only one who didn't quite look like she stepped out of a painting. Her platinum blond hair was styled in crinkly waves, feathering out of a loosely placed blue satin veil. It was the shiniest type of satin, reflecting the white twinkle lights with a bright shine. She wore enough mascara to ward off ninjas and her lips were painted a fire engine red.

Lois went on. "And her husband! Poor fella. Just look at how tired he is."

"Which one is he?" I asked. "Let me guess. Joseph?" The scowly one.

"Yup." She lowered her voice for dramatic effect. "Nine kids. Baby Jesus makes ten."

"Yikes." Georgia winced.

I laughed. "And I thought I came from a big family."

"How about you two?" asked Lois, wagging her brows at us. "Any children?"

"Us?" Georgia exclaimed, half laughing. "No."

"Why not?"

Hmmm, maybe because we'd known each other for less than forty-eight hours? Strangely enough, it didn't feel like that. It was almost as though Georgia had always been in my life, tucked away in that dormant part of my heart. And now here she was, smiling and laughing. Being radiant.

Georgia turned her gaze to me. There was softness in her eyes communicating a deep thought. My chest filled with warmth as we stood there, eyes fixed on each other. Georgia's lovely lips parted. She wanted to say something. Maybe answer Lois' question. But Lois had moved along down the line without us noticing.

How long were we staring at each other like that?

"Shall we?" I asked, offering Georgia my hand.

"We shall." She laced her fingers through mine, lazily strolling with me. Even through our gloves my skin burned from her touch. Electricity shot up my arm, jolting my heart to a gallop. Perhaps she felt my reaction because she squeezed my hand tighter, inclining her body closer as we walked.

We followed the crowd around the corner of the great barn where everyone gathered to listen to the combined adult and children's choirs. They had just started the most beautiful rendition of *O Holy Night*. Harmonies soared to our ears accompanied by pre-recorded orchestrations. The sound was full and powerful—how I imagined a true choir of angles would sound. I couldn't imagine the moment could be more perfect but then it began to snow and the heavenly experience was complete. Soft, white flakes descended upon us, dancing with a feathery glow as they reflected the Christmas lights. Georgia's features gleamed.

She smiled, watching the choir perform while snowflakes landed on her hair to form a halo. I'd never seen anything so angelic in my life. And all I wanted to do in that moment was to absorb her in my arms and brush my lips against hers.

A brisk gust of wind swept over us and she shuddered.

"Do you want to go inside?" I asked.

She nodded, letting go of my hand to pull her coat tighter around her neck. I guided her through the door with a hand at the small of her back. She shuddered again. I hoped that time it wasn't from the cold.

Inside, several people gathered around the refreshment table. Children walked away carrying plates piled high with cookies and cakes. It was like a competition amongst themselves.

The child among us with the largest dessert mountain wins a tummy ache. Hazzah!

We stood back, waiting for the sugar mob to disperse. Most everyone had come inside now. I noticed Teresa laughing with a couple of the beige skirt ladies. They were chatting and smiling, full of Christmas cheer. This town had a way of bringing that out in a person.

"Should we get in line for some sweets?"

Georgia shook her head in response. "I want to, but I fear for my life."

"Are you sure? It might be our last meal for a long time. We could stuff our pockets with Lois' fudge and make a run for it."

"Don't forget the banana bread." She giggled, turning a few heads. She was magnetic like that.

Teresa noticed us from across the room and waved. We waved back. That's how it goes when you know exactly two people in town. Three, if we're counting the gravy lady.

She hugged her friends in parting and came over to talk to us. There was a lot of hugging going on in this town.

"What did you think of the nativity?" Teresa asked.

"Absolutely gorgeous," said Georgia. "It was the coolest thing ever."

Teresa beamed. "Ever? Wow, that's quite the endorsement."

She thanked us again for helping in the kitchen, inviting us to an after-hours party of sorts.

"It's just some friends getting together at the Light Hope Cafe. Hot apple cider is on the house."

She explained how the old cafe was going under when Hope Church took over and saved the business, changing the name. They served sandwiches and coffee but drew in a good crowd of folks after dark for the open mic night every Wednesday.

"It's a good way to witness to those in town who want to go somewhere at night besides the bar," she explained. "But tonight it's a private event for all our volunteers."

I exchanged a look with Georgia. I was silently saying *Christmas miracles all around*. She was probably thinking *Why not? We have no other options*.

Both were true. But I had faith it would all work out.

"We'd love to go," said Georgia.

"Perfect. I just need to help my husband clean up and I'll see you there."

"You need some help?" I asked.

"Oh, how nice. I could ask him." She scanned the room, looking for her husband I supposed. "There he is, talking with the Sisters. I'll give him a minute."

She pointed to the sweet ladies she was talking to earlier. They were in an animated conversation with Pastor Kevin.

Georgia raised her brows. "I didn't know you're the pastor's wife. He's a really good speaker."

I wondered how Georgia could know what kind of speaker the pastor was with Lois chatting in her ear the whole time. But

I had to agree the man had a strong stage presence. Tall and confident. Plus, he seemed like a straight up guy.

"Who are those women?" I couldn't resist asking. "Did you say they're his sisters?"

They didn't look like they could be his sisters. One was olive-skinned with dark hair and the other was much older while Kevin was a forty-something guys who looked like he stepped right off the Scottish Highlands.

"Not *his* sisters," Teresa explained. "They're the Sisters from the Sacred Heart Convent. They run a charity house about ten miles from here."

Nuns. Boy was I way off.

Georgia giggled. "Wyatt thought they were candy shop employees."

"It was a good guess," I cried defensively. "Nuns make chocolate, don't they?"

"You're thinking about wine," Georgia said.

"Oh yeah."

"So that's Sister Edna with the salt and pepper hair." Teresa nodded in their direction. "And the younger one is Sister Patty. The other Sisters are scattered about. They're the ones who donated all that turkey. They make a trip once a week to bring food for the poor."

Georgia's eyes glistened. "That's so wonderful. I think it's awesome how you all work together for the community. I'm not used to seeing that kind of generosity in the world."

The few last words got caught in her throat. She was deeply touched. Whether it was the people, the soup kitchen, the living nativity, or just exhaustion, I couldn't tell. But something lit up Georgia's expression and she had that squishy, doughy look about her—like she was ready to turn into a puddle.

Teresa wrapped her hands around Georgia's shoulders and

looked into her eyes with a soft smile. "You could if you look hard enough, sweetheart. There's kindness everywhere."

Oh no. I sensed a cry fest coming on.

Watch out gentlemen, the feels have been set free.

Aaaand then of course...they hugged.

"You two go on," said Teresa dabbing her eye. "We've got the teenagers to help clean up. They need service hours to graduate high school."

We set out for the long walk back into town but before we left we raided the dessert table and wrapped plenty of fudge and banana bread in napkins.

We hadn't made it far down the road before Georgia burst into peels of laughter.

"What? What's so funny?"

"You. And Reeses in that manger."

"That was kinda funny, wasn't it?"

She took my arm, pressing into me as we walked along. "There's never a dull moment with you, Charlie Brown."

Good grief.

16

WYATT

The return trip into town wasn't exactly a romantic stroll. The road seemed to stretch on like in those nightmares where your destination gets farther and farther away the more you walk.

The crisp evening chill had turned to a harsh, biting cold. I just about lost feeling in my feet and Reeses' bag was getting heavier by the second. I knew Georgia was frozen. Her winter coat and boots were more fashionable than practical. Which would have been fine in New York. And pointless in Los Angeles. I wondered how warm it was there. A frigid 72 degrees? I could have been poolside drinking an iced tea at this very moment if our plane hadn't been detoured. I wouldn't have been robbed of all my stuff. My clothes, my money, my laptop.

But I'd be alone.

With Georgia, none of those things mattered. What would I have, really? A few measly possessions and a cheap Hollywood news story I felt sleazy about. There was no way I could do it now. As soon as I could charge my phone I'd call my friend and tell him the deal was off.

And what about Georgia? She was right. I was a walking

disaster. Charlie Brown to the power of ten. There was no way she'd ever consider a guy like me. She belonged in her beautiful life sipping champagne and getting massages—or however the rich and famous spend their time. Not freezing on a rural road with the likes of me.

Somehow I'd get her home. I didn't know how, but I vowed to do whatever it took. A silent prayer left my heart.

Please, help me get her home safely.

Not three seconds later an old Winnebago rambled up the road from seemingly out of nowhere. It wasn't going fast, but passed us before coming to a stop a few hundred feet ahead. It stood there for a couple of seconds and then lurched into reverse, the tires slugging through the thick snow.

At first I thought it might hit us, the way the driver swerved and fishtailed and Georgia and I ran off the road. But then the RV straightened its trajectory and skidded to a stop right before reaching us.

The rear door opened and a warm light shone from the inside. There was some chatter and then a young woman leaned out waving us over.

"Come on before you freeze."

As we approached, and her silhouette gave way to reveal her face, we saw that she was that nun who Teresa was talking to earlier.

Georgia and I didn't know what to say so we climbed into the RV.

"I'm Sister Patty." She hugged us, which we were used to by now. As she closed the door behind us, an acoustic guitar rang a chord and all dozen nuns inside the RV sang a short welcome song to the tune of Kumbaya.

WELCOME IN, *my friends, welcome in.*

Oh, friends, welcome in.

THEN SISTER PATTY went around introducing the other Sisters. I couldn't remember all their names, so no doubt Georgia was secretly assigning classical composer monikers to them all. The one with the guitar was easy to remember. Her name was Paula.

"I'm Wyatt and this is Georgia." I made a little bow not sure of the correct protocol for greeting a Winnebago full of nuns. "And this here's Reeses."

We found an empty spot to sit and the RV heaved with a jerk. A few skids of the tires screeched beneath us, then a pitch forward, jolting us in our seats and we were on our way. I let Reeses roam about and he became the center of attention. Rock star status.

"Are you going to the cafe?" Sister Patty asked Georgia.

"Yes."

She smiled. "We're going there, too."

Then Sister Edna, the older one Teresa was talking to, asked, "What made you two decide to walk back to town in this weather? Did something happen to your car?"

"You could say that," I said with an ironic tone.

Something in her face, and in all those faces actually, told me they really wanted to know. So Georgia and I gave them the truncated version of our story from the beginning, taking turns telling them of our adventures. It was eerie how we finished each other's sentences.

Sister Edna listened intently and smiled sweetly when we got to the part where we helped serve the turkey dinner.

"And so you found your way to Bethlehem. Like Mary and Joseph."

"Yeah. And there's no room at the inn," I joked.

Georgia elbowed me reproachfully.

"Well, these things have a way of working out," said Sister Edna. "There's no such thing as a coincidence."

"Only a God-incidence," added Sister Patty.

The RV lumbered on, going extra slow. Whoever was driving was being extra careful. Reeses was in belly rub heaven, and the cheerful women seemed more than happy to dole out all the attention his little doggie heart desired. They certainly didn't fit the penguin suit stereotype I was used to. Most of them were in their twenties and thirties—young and fresh-faced. And all of them were full of laughter.

So, partly because I felt some instant connection with these ladies, and partly because of my burning curiosity, I said, "Don't take this the wrong way, but you don't look like nuns."

Sister Edna raised a brow. "Because we don't have the traditional habit?"

Georgia face-palmed. "Wyatt!"

"It's okay," said Sister Patty. "We get asked this all the time."

"What's a habit?" I asked. "The black and white veil thing?"

"You've probably seen pictures of Mother Teresa," said Sister Patty. "Her order wears blue stripes. Some orders wear black and white. Some wear brown. We wear something a little more simple."

"A habit is more of a promise to God than an article of clothing," explained Sister Edna. "Our order was founded during the time of the Nazis. The Sisters then couldn't wear a traditional habit because of persecution and threat of arrest. And so we wear a habit of fidelity, of joy, of love. A habit of caring for each other and for the community."

That explained the inner glow these women had.

Georgia smiled. "I like that."

"Me too," said Sister Patty. "That's what called me to serve."

"We're here!" the driver called out. She had light brown hair and extremely rosy cheeks. She skidded the Winnebago to a stop and put it in park, waving at us through the rear view mirror.

"That's Sister Ruth," said Patty. "Come on. Let's get some hot apple cider."

The party was well under way inside the cafe. It was already packed before we walked in, but somehow everyone shifted around and we were a comfortable crowd.

A stout woman served the hot apple cider from behind the bar. We later learned her name was Hannah, the original owner of the cafe. She still ran the place as before but now had the financial backing of Hope Church.

The cider was crazy good.

"Wow. What did they put in this stuff?" said Georgia. "Unicorn tears?"

Pastor Kevin and Teresa arrived soon after. Their daughter, Joy, had changed out of her Mary costume and found a corner of the cafe to bury herself in her cell phone.

Hannah set out trays of hot mini donuts on every table and counter. They were amazing morsels of fried dough and powdered sugar. I must have eaten a dozen.

Upbeat Christmas hits played from the speaker system and those not engaged in lively conversation were dancing. At one point, Lois snagged me by the arm for a dance. I hadn't even seen her walk in; then again the place was pretty packed. Georgia's smiling face disappeared through the crowd of dancers as I was pulled away. She laughed and gave an encouraging clap.

I couldn't find her for ten or fifteen minutes, and when I did, she was under the threshold that led to the restrooms. She was smiling, but there was a hint of worry on her features.

"Hey, what's wrong?"

She leaned against the frame and sighed. "Tomorrow's Christmas Eve. And we have no way of getting to California."

"I know." In an effort to comfort her, I caressed her arms. "But we'll get there somehow."

She shifted under the weight of my hands and focused on me. "There's something I didn't tell you. I don't *just* need to get home in time for Christmas. My brother's getting married and he's trying to keep it low key. I really need to be there."

I parted my lips, wanting to say something in response. But I was afraid my features would betray me. I already knew about the wedding. If I were to act surprised, she'd see right through me. Instead, I drew her into my arms and nuzzled my nose in her hair, inhaling her shampoo. It still held a trace of that strawberry scent but it was now mixed with a hint of pine and ash.

"I'll do everything in my power to get you home on time," I whispered into her soft locks. "I promise."

She broke away from the hug just enough to see my eyes. Her warm, lovely face was only an inch away and the cinnamon in her sweet breath brushed against my senses. My heart hammered in my chest as she curled up the corners of her lips in a honey-laden smile. Her eyes danced. They met my gaze in wonder and then flickered up to a sprig of mistletoe dangling above our heads.

I may have read somewhere that it was bad luck not to kiss if you find yourselves under mistletoe. Or maybe I made that up. Either way, I wasn't about to tempt the Christmas fairies.

I lowered my lips, just a millimeter, as if asking permission. She quivered under my touch. Her breath snagged in response —in anticipation. And as I closed the gap, a wish hung between us as though, through the magic of a mistletoe kiss, every worry would melt away and our Christmas dreams would come true.

A loud *pop* ricocheted through the cafe followed by gasps and complete darkness. Georgia jolted back. The music cut off and was replaced by murmurs and various voices rumbling, "What happened?"

"The power went out."

A strong, male voice said, "Everybody remain calm. I'll check the breaker box."

Cell phones fired up in a blue hue and in a matter of minutes, candles illuminated the cafe in a soft, warm glow.

I glanced back to see Georgia biting her bottom lip, her features cast in darkness but still betraying a hint of disappointment. I shouldn't have hesitated. And now the moment was gone.

17

GEORGIA

A few people freaked out when the power went out. I was too dazed by Wyatt's lips *almost* touching mine to notice much of anything for several minutes.

I had to get it together. I didn't do hookups with guys I barely knew. But why did Wyatt feel so familiar? Two days ago he didn't exist. Now he was just there, taking residence in my life like it's the most natural thing in the world. And I liked it.

Pastor Kevin announced in his booming voice, "There's a downed power line just outside the cafe. Also the storm is coming in pretty strong right now. I recommend everyone stay put for now."

This was followed by some groans and some talking all at once. Kevin held up his hands to quiet the racket.

"I called Eric at the fire station. He's sending some guys, don't worry. In the mean time, Hanna and Teresa are putting out sandwiches. On the house."

Everyone went back to mumbling amongst themselves, making the most of the situation. It was still a party—just a mellow one. And maybe a tad drab. So I sprang into action.

I'd noticed an upright piano when we first walked in. As a

musician, my eyes can't help but latch on to instruments, even through a crowd of people. What this party needed was music. Luckily, I knew a tune or two.

Wyatt followed me over.

"Where are you going?"

I grinned, scrunching my nose at him. "Just over here to liven things up a bit."

My fingers flew over the keys playing *Große Sonate für das Hammerklavier* as effortlessly as some people excel at typing or making piecrust. Wyatt gaped at me incredulously.

"What is that?"

I kept playing. "Beethoven."

He laughed, shaking his head.

I narrowed my eyes. "What?"

"I may be Charlie Brown, but you're Schroeder."

I hitched one shoulder up and played on. The party guests turned and stared like they weren't sure what to make of me. I spotted Reeses on top of a high-top table, ears at attention.

"Reeses likes it," I said. "He's got good taste in music."

Wyatt's face was all wonder. "How is it I'm just finding out you play piano?"

"I guess I'm full of all sorts of surprises," I replied.

"Know any Christmas tunes?"

Do I know any Christmas tunes?!

"Is Santa fat and jolly?" I wagged my brows. "Here's one for you, Charlie Brown."

I transitioned smoothly into *Linus and Lucy*, otherwise known as the *Peanuts Theme Song*. Wyatt scooped up Reeses and began dancing, bobbing up and down like the cartoon. People started to join in. It was crazy fun. I played one Christmas song after another. At one point, someone put an empty mason jar on the piano lid and stuffed a five-dollar bill inside. I started taking requests.

Silver Bells, Deck the Halls, Let it Snow. More cash tips filled the jar. Most of the songs were carols everyone joined in on but a few people requested stuff like *Santa Baby* or *Have Yourself a Merry Little Christmas* which turned out to be more like Karaoke.

"I have a request," said Wyatt. "Sing a duet with me?"

I waved him off. "I can't sing."

"Neither can I. We'll be terrible together. Come on. For Reeses?" He squeezed Reeses to his cheek to play the cute card.

"Oh, okay. But I warned you. I'm not a great singer."

"I'll be the judge of that."

The song he wanted was *Baby It's Cold Outside,* so I started in, cringing as my voice left my mouth. Wyatt's face brightened as if I had the most beautiful voice in the world. I was convinced he must have been deaf.

He joined in, playing up the comedy. He was making up his own words, giving everyone a good laugh. More money piled in our jar. He kicked it up a notch, inspired by the tips. We were on a roll, singing our little hearts out. He had a pretty good voice. I mean, he was no Pavarotti but I certainly didn't hold a candle to the many fantastic vocalists at my school. But Wyatt was wonderful in his own Wyatt way. His eyes glistened as he leaned toward me, singing about how my lips looked delicious.

Gah.

I thanked my lucky stars he couldn't see the bright red tinge on my cheeks in the candlelight. What would people think if he stole a kiss right then and there? How would I react? Would I kiss him back?

He really did have a dazzling smile. It wasn't just because of his perfectly straight, gleaming white teeth, or how those kissable lips formed into a scrumptious crescent. Or even how his eyes flashed in such a way, they sent bolts of lightning to my belly button.

I discovered as I sat there playing piano, singing a duet with Wyatt, that his smile was stunning because it sprouted from deep within—from a place so pure and so real, it was almost blinding.

A flutter built inside of me, filling me to the brim. My heart thundered in my chest. So. Darn. Loud. So overwhelming. My fingers faltered, fumbling over the keys. Wyatt's smile only grew wider.

I braced myself for another wave—the falling sensation that's equal measures frightening and thrilling. Like a roller coaster—the kind that drops you down so your stomach leaps into your throat.

Was this what it was like to fall in love? This beautiful ache burning me to embers. The awareness in my entire body responding to Wyatt's presence like static cling on socks.

No.

People didn't fall in love overnight. That only happened in movies.

In a flash, the power blasted back on—the lights, the music, the donut machine all coming to life at once. Everyone cheered and applauded when the crew responsible for restoring the power ambled inside. Hannah ushered them to the bar to offer them food. Our heroes. We were saved.

A moment later, I felt Teresa's hand on my shoulder.

"A little elf told me you two need a place to stay tonight," she said.

Hmmm. I wondered who that might be.

Kevin came over and greeted us with a handshake. The only one in town not into hugs, it seemed.

"We want you to stay at our house tonight," he said in his low baritone. "And we won't take no for an answer."

I'D NEVER BEEN MORE grateful for a hot shower in my life. Teresa lent me some pajamas that dragged on the floor when I walked so I ended up tying little knots at the hem of the pants. I slept on Joy's trundle bed. She was under the impression we were having a slumber party and was all about the girl-talk late into the night. She asked so many questions. Was Wyatt my boyfriend? Was he a good kisser? What was my longest Snapchat streak?

We kinda bonded.

In the morning I found my clothes washed and folded. Was there no end to these people's kindness? Wyatt greeted me in the kitchen bright-faced and clean-shaven. Apparently the sofa he slept on was even better than the backseat of that Mustang.

He'd already taken Reeses out to do his business and the little dog was nibbling on some chicken on a paper plate.

Wyatt gazed at me. "Last night was something else, wasn't it?"

"Which part?"

"All of it. I feel...happy. You know what I mean?"

"Yeah. I think so." I eyed the spread on the kitchen island. Pastries, fruit, coffee, and a note for us to help ourselves.

Wyatt poured a cup of coffee and handed it to me. "Where did you learn to play piano like that? Is music your major?"

"Yes."

"That's awesome." He poured another cup and leaned next to me on the counter. "What school do you go to? NYU?"

"Juilliard." I bit into a cheese danish.

"Of course you do."

I winked at him as I chewed my danish. This all felt so natural, like we were playing house.

Silly.

"So, we should probably figure out a way to get to L.A. in the next twenty-four hours," he said, running his fingers though his locks. Seriously, he could do that all day and I'd never tire of watching him. "Any ideas?"

"Hang on." I padded to the coat rack and unzipped the inside pocket, bringing a pile of cash back into the kitchen. "Our tips."

His eyes widened. "You mean *your* tips. How much did you make?"

I straightened out the bills, stacking them on the counter. "I dunno. Help me count."

We each took a stack and counted silently. There were mostly ones, but also quite a few fives and a couple twenties.

"Wow. I counted fifty-seven," said Wyatt. "What about you?"

"Eighty-four. That can't be right."

Wyatt began counting on his fingers. Fifty-seven and eighty-four...that's...how much?"

"I don't math this early," I joked.

"A hundred and forty-one," a deep voice answered. Kevin sauntered into the kitchen dressed in jeans and a flannel. He poured a cup of coffee and joined us at the island. "Good morning. Sleep well?"

We both replied that we did and thanked him profusely, especially for taking the time to wash our clothes.

He waved off our gushing. "It's all my bride's doing. She's the greatest lady I know."

"I don't suppose we could find a really fast train that can get us to California for a hundred and forty-one bucks?" I said, squinting at Wyatt.

The ding of the doorbell echoed through the house and footsteps pounded down the stairs.

"I got it." Teresa ran to the front door. She was a blur as she whizzed by the kitchen archway.

Kevin polished off his coffee in one swig and rinsed his cup in the sink. "Let's all go see who that is."

He walked out, expecting us to follow him. I couldn't possibly imagine who might be at their door that'd care to meet Wyatt and me, but figured this was their cute small town custom.

Let's all say hello to the Fed-Ex guy. Hugs for everyone.

But unless the Fed-Ex uniform was a beige skirt and white blouse, the visitors at the door were definitely not delivering a package. Or so I thought.

Sisters Edna, Patty, and Ruth floated in, all smiles and cheerful greetings and hugged us all. It was so nice to see them again.

"Where's your lovely daughter?" asked Edna.

Teresa took their coats. "Sleeping. You know how teenagers are."

I certainly did after last night. No wonder the chatty little thing was tired.

Kevin invited them into the living room. "Can I offer you some coffee or juice?"

"Oh no, thank you." Sister Edna sat on the sofa as we all found seats. "I'm just here to ask a favor of Georgia and Wyatt."

That was surprising.

Wyatt almost jumped with enthusiasm. "Anything. Just name it."

"Good." Sister Edna sat up straight. "Regarding the RV Sister Ruth here drove us in last night."

Sister Ruth threaded her fingers on her lap. "Tried to drive."

"You did a fine job," said Sister Patty, covering her hand with encouragement.

"Yes, well." Sister Edna continued. "Our sisters in the Costa Mesa convent are in need of the vehicle. They have a lot more retreats and need the RV for trips up to the mountains. There's a retreat center at Big Bear Lake."

I was familiar with Big Bear. My dad took us there when I was a little girl. "It's beautiful up there," I said.

Edna agreed. "It certainly is. But we only need to take the RV as far as Costa Mesa. We had planned on taking the trip after the Epiphany, but it's quite a long drive."

"So long," Ruth agreed.

"We weren't really looking forward to it," added Patty. "At all."

Sister Edna focused on Wyatt and me. "And now God has provided a solution."

Ruth dangled a set of keys. "You would be doing us a great favor."

"Wait. I don't follow." Wyatt shook his head.

Kevin jumped in. "They have a camper that needs to get to California. You happen to be going that way but don't have wheels."

"It's perfect," exclaimed Teresa.

"But, you would trust us with your camper?" I asked. "Just like that?"

Edna shrugged. "Eh. It's insured."

18

GEORGIA

The proud part of me wanted to refuse the motor home. I wasn't accustomed to accepting charity. The nuns insisted it was they who were indebted to us for the favor, but we all knew it was a pure act of kindness on their part. After some resistance, I finally accepted the offer. It was...humbling. They even gave us gas money.

"We're saving thousands of dollars on return airfare," said Sister Edna. "Take it."

She shoved it in Wyatt's hands and wouldn't let him give it back.

As we pulled out of town I vowed to pay them back and then some.

"Do you know what roads to take?" I asked Wyatt. "We don't have a GPS."

I wanted to add that he didn't have the best track record, but I kept my lips zipped.

"Kevin gave me very specific directions and Sister Ruth said there's a road map in the glove box."

"Alright. You drive, I'll navigate. And as soon as we get to a major city, we'll get you a phone charger."

I popped the glove box to find the map, but the most prominent item inside was a gold manila envelope with our names on it.

"You've got to be kidding."

Wyatt glanced over, still keeping one eye on the road. "What?"

"There's four hundred dollars in here and a note that reads *Just in case we couldn't convince you to accept the gas money earlier*. Turn around. We're returning this."

"We can't turn back, now. We're on the highway. You wanna get lost?"

"No, I certainly do not," I cried.

"Okay then. You said you wanted to pay them back, let's just add this to the amount we owe them and that's that."

"I guess."

It occurred to me then, how Wyatt's understanding of my wealth must have been grossly inflated. Sure, I had a movie star brother. But that was him. Not me.

"I'm not the rich girl you think I am."

Wyatt quickly proclaimed, "I am all about paying my share. I promise. Even if I have to take three jobs."

"No, it's not about that. I'm not penniless. Well, technically I was last night, but that's beside the point. I just don't want you to think I'm like that evil ex-girlfriend of yours."

He laughed. "I don't think that."

"The truth is, yes, my brother is ludicrously rich. But I don't like taking handouts from him. I earn my own money playing concerts, recording with orchestras, that sort of thing."

"You *should* make money playing piano. You're really good."

"Thanks. But I don't have piles of Benjamins lying around my apartment. I play a couple of gigs a month and I get by."

He nodded, concentrating on his driving duties. "So you don't make it rain like the rappers do in those music videos?"

"I know I look the type, but no."

"Well that's disappointing."

We rode along, me making sure we were on the right track, he whistling Christmas tunes. It was strange how I felt weirdly close to him yet knew very little about his life. Was I just fooling myself?

"What about you?" I asked, the question burning through me. "Tell me about that rich girl. What made her evil? Besides being rich. That one's obvious."

Wyatt hesitated, quietly thinking of the right words to answer my tactlessly intrusive question.

"Never mind. Sorry I asked. I'm too nosey."

"No, no. It's fine." He raked his fingers through his hair, a habit I was rapidly growing fond of. "It's just where do I begin? There were the horns. I guess that was a red flag right there."

"Oooh. That would be a deal breaker for me," I deadpanned.

"Yeah, well...I was young and gave my heart away too freely. Totally my fault."

"I can relate to that."

"Yeah?" He flashed a blinding side smile. "Anyway, I could never figure out why she never wanted to be seen with me. When I'd ask her to go to the movies or out somewhere with friends, she would say she wanted me all to herself. Turned out she was just slumming it for kicks. I found out she was dating some society dude at the same time."

"Ouch." My heart went out to him.

"So I crashed one of her dad's fancy parties to confront her. And she looked down her nose at me and just majorly insulted me in front of everyone. I knew a lot of the college students there. I thought they were my friends. But they just laughed."

"I'm so sorry. That *is* evil."

He took a fortifying breath and shook it all out of him like it was that easy to toss the memory aside. I wanted to reach out and touch him. Show him some comfort.

"You wanna know why my brother is so protective?" I asked after a minute.

"I know why," he said. "Because he's an older brother and he loves you. Simple."

Not as simple as he thought.

"I gave my heart away, too," I admitted. "Except I was a lot younger. Jorge was a family friend, practically a brother. When my dad died, Jorge got into a big fight with Will. I didn't understand it all so I rebelled. I'd go meet him behind my brother's back, text him all the time. I guess I developed a tiny crush but was too naive to do anything about it."

"Was he a lot older?"

"Only about five years. But that's a lot when you're a teenager."

Wyatt clenched the steering wheel tighter, already angry on my behalf for something that happened years ago. "So what happened? Did he break your heart?"

"In a way. I found out the hard way he was only using me to get back at my brother. Then he snuck into my room late one night—completely strung out on who-knows-what."

The veins in Wyatt's neck grew taut and his nostrils flared when he said, "Did he take advantage of you, Georgia?" There was vengeance in his voice.

"No. Calm down, Thor. My brother saved me. Actually, it was our dog, Lady. If it wasn't for her barking..."

"I can't wait to meet your dog. And I'm not gonna lie. I'd like to meet your brother, too."

I laughed. "You will."

"So, the guy—Jorge—did he go to jail?"

I sighed, remembering how long it took for Jorge to screw up bad enough for any charges to stick. "Eventually."

It wasn't until my brother met Beth—when her then-roommate fell victim to Jorge. Will went to Mexico to track him down. It was years later than I'd hoped, but at least now Jorge couldn't hurt anybody ever again.

Moving on. I was ready to change the subject.

"Slug bug." I punched the air between us because I couldn't reach Wyatt's arm.

"What?"

"Slug bug. You don't know that game? When you see a Volkswagen bug—"

"I know the game," he interrupted. "But there hasn't been another car for miles. Let alone a VW."

"I was just getting us started. Want some fudge?" I dipped into my pocket for the napkin of treats I slipped from the church. Wyatt had his own stash, but I figured we'd raid his pockets later.

"Heck yeah. Don't hold out on me." He took a hand off the wheel to reach out for some fudge. I swatted it.

"Just keep driving and try to stay on the road this time."

"Yes, ma'am, Miss Darcy."

WE TRAVELED for several hours singing Christmas carols, devouring fudge and A.J.'s banana bread (which was uh-may-ZING) and reminisced about our favorite gifts from Santa. Mine was a dollhouse. Wyatt's was a Navajo drum. It was the best thing ever to take a peek into Wyatt's life. He spoke freely about his hopes and dreams, how he switched majors too many times to count, and all the spec screenplays he'd written but tucked away in a file never to see the light of day. I encouraged him to dust them off and send them out.

"Ya never know until you try," I said, wagging a finger.

We stopped a few times to let Reeses out, filled the tank, and grabbed lunch at a super market. We weren't about to take any more chances at roadside diners.

Wyatt studied the map at one of our stops, spreading it out on the kitchenette table. "If we continue to drive with minimal stops we can get to L.A. by six or seven in the morning."

"That's nuts," I said, shaking my head. "We'll have to rest for a few hours."

"Are you sure? What about the wedding?"

"It's at four PM," I assured him. "We'll be okay."

After the adventure we'd had so far, even *I* didn't believe my own words. But what could be done at this point? I closed my hand over his and gave a comforting squeeze. He jerked his head to meet my gaze, his features alight with awareness. He was so beautiful. I bit my bottom lip to keep my jaw from coming unhinged and his focus instinctively dipped to my mouth then back to focus on my eyes.

I'd never wanted a kiss in my life more than I did just then. I wanted more than a kiss. I wanted everything about Wyatt—the smiles, the small touches, the quirky conversation. I'd even take the zany disasters as long as I could be near him. I channeled all my energy to convey my desire for a kiss in my lazy gaze. What was that come-hither look the heroine always made in my brother's movies? Hooded eyes? Ah yes. I dropped my lids to half-mast, trying not to blink. My lashes fluttered. So sexy. I had him now.

"Are you okay?" He grimaced. "You look really tired."

"Tired? No. A little cold, maybe." I tried the pouty lips next. "I wonder if you could...warm me up?"

He blinked at me. "Why don't you climb in the back and get in the bed?"

"The *bed?!*"

Yikes, I better dial the sexy back a notch.

"Yeah. Crawl under the blankets and I'll wake you up when we make our next stop." He pranced to the front of the camper and slid in the driver's seat, whistling *Jingle Bells*. I eyed Reeses who had his little tongue dangling out of his snout, the corners of his doggie mouth upturned. He was totally laughing at me.

"Do *you* wanna kiss me?"

He yipped and wagged his tail.

"All right. Come along." I slugged to the back of the RV and planted myself on the bed. Come to think of it, I *was* kind of drowsy. Joy kept me up most of the night showing me trending Tik Toks until my eyeballs bled.

Kids these days.

I snuggled under the covers, lifting them up to my chin as Reeses rested his head on my shoulder—his furry whiskers tickling my cheek. The camper rocked into motion and before we drove onto the highway, the soothing rhythm lulled me to sleep.

19

GEORGIA

I woke with a start as the RV bounced over the bumpy road. Disoriented and groggy, it took a minute to remember where I was. I'd slept so heavily, I didn't notice when we left the main highway onto rural streets. I peeked out the back curtain. Rural terrain stretched on as jagged rocks glowed red with the last tinge of the setting sun. Snow-capped mountains stood watch in the distance, safeguarding the dry, uneven foothills dotted with patches of white.

"Where are we?" I stumbled the length of the RV, taming the tangles in my hair.

"New Mexico," Wyatt chirped.

Reeses was in my seat, the traitor. He perched his front paws on the windowsill so he could see outside and his tail was going a mile a minute. He was so jumpy and excited. I scooped him up and reclaimed my seat as we rolled onto a dirt road passing huge wooden posts, which appeared as though they had once been part of a great fence. The serpentine road, pocked with dips and craggy rocks, weaved through small hills and inclined gently into a forest of odd-looking pines. The RV rocked and swayed as we rambled up the road, reaching a stretch of farmland resembling an old ranch. It could have been a scene from an old western if it weren't for the gleaming red Chevy parked below the steps of a stunning flat-roofed adobe house.

Wyatt parked the RV and grinned at me, his teeth dazzling across his face.

"We're here."

"Where's *here* exactly?"

Reeses went ballistic. He leapt off my lap and bounded over to Wyatt, scratching on the driver's side window.

"Okay, already. Calm down peanut."

The crazy little dog shook all over like he couldn't stand being inside the RV a second more. How long had the poor thing been holding it?

Wyatt cracked the door and Reeses bolted. I didn't see where he went at first, guessing he'd found a tree to baptize, but then he came into view galloping up the steps toward the house, barking all the way.

"Wow, he's really gone bonkers. Did he find a squirrel?'

Wyatt reached over and tucked a stray lock of hair behind my ear, grazing his knuckles along my cheek as he retracted his hand.

"Come on before he gets into too much trouble."

He spun his legs around and hopped out onto the gravel, closing the door behind him.

"Wait! Wyatt. What is this place?"

He didn't hear me. He was already heading up, two steps at a time.

I stumbled out to join him, still not completely awake until the cold hit me. I turned right back around to get our coats.

The house stood prominently on high ground with stone steps leading to a gravel footpath. Desert brush and cacti lined the walkways and served as ground cover. And the whole area was lit up by luminaries.

When I caught up, Wyatt was waiting for me at the top landing of the steps. He reached out as I approached, not for the coat, even though I handed it to him, but for my hand. He leveled his gaze on me, filling his chest with the crisp air, and ran his thumb over my wrist. The most peaceful wave ran though me, and there with a backdrop of the deep blue sky and the warm paper bag lights, he glowed. Beyond real, in a Photoshop sort of way.

"Wyatt? Is that you?" An older woman called excitedly, running down the footpath. "Good heavens!"

She was a petite, slender woman in her fifties with cropped auburn hair, wire rimmed glasses and the friendliest smile imaginable. She had a free, salt-of-the earth quality. Reeses ran in circles around her as she hurried along, wiping her hands on her apron. Wyatt met her halfway and threw his arms around her, squeezing her for a long moment.

"I can't believe you're here," she said through tears. "Home for Christmas. Let me look at you."

She held his shoulders at arm's length, which wasn't very far for her. She had to crane her neck to see his face.

"Ma, I want you to meet someone," he said, turning his eyes to me. She wiped her cheeks and shifted to look at me. Her whole face lit up and a bright smile spread wide across her features.

"Is this the one?" she said, beaming at me.

The one?

"Hi, I'm Georgia." I closed the distance and offered my hand. She brushed it aside and swooped in for a hug.

"Wyatt's told me so much about you," she said, breaking the hug to squeeze my hands. "You're even prettier than he described."

"Ma!"

I had no idea how *pretty* I looked at present considering my bed head and the dried up drool in the corner of my mouth. Also, I was fairly certain I had pillow marks on my face.

"Uh, thanks?"

She scrunched up her nose adorably. "Let's get you two inside. I was just about to make biscochitos."

We followed her up to the house, our path illuminated by the paper bag lanterns, each one with a flaming votive candle inside. They were everywhere—even covering the perimeter of the roof. It was one of the most spectacular sights I'd ever seen.

"Should we be worried about a fire hazard?" I whispered to Wyatt.

"Nah. She lights these every Christmas Eve." He lifted my hand and pressed his lips to my knuckles. "It's tradition."

Heaven help me, those lips were even more velvety than they looked. I turned to goo right then and there.

He tucked my hand in the crook of his elbow and pointed out areas of interest like a proud tour guide:

These agave plants have been here for seventy-five years.

And:

My great-grandpa built this house with his bare hands. He formed every adobe brick out of mud and hay.

It was all so beautiful and fascinating. The inside of the house was adorned with a mixture of Spanish and Native American decor. Cast iron sconces flanked a mantle made of reclaimed wood, the floor was a terra cotta tile, dried red chili peppers hung in wreaths in the archways, and colorful water color paintings of men in feathered headdresses or dark-haired beauties adorned every wall.

Wyatt's mother was a work of art herself. She wore a pink western button down with fringe pockets, a woven vest with embroidered orange doves, and enough turquoise jewelry to

DRIVING MISS DARCY

open a shop on eBay. She wasted no time in serving up some hot cocoa and planted us on the sofa right in front of the fireplace. Reeses made himself at home on the rug.

"Thank you, Mrs. Silva." I blew on the cup, enjoying the warm steam on my face.

"Oh, please, call me Anita. Most of my children do. Except for Wyatt." She winked at him. I got the sense he was her favorite, even though no mother would admit such a thing.

"Your sisters will be so surprised." She leaned over and draped her hand on Wyatt's knee. "Palanca and Steven are coming. You won't recognize Sophia, she's almost two, and if she stays awake at Mass, we'll let her open one present."

"Palanca's your sister?"

Wyatt nodded. "Yeah. Listen, Ma—"

"Janet and Jennifer," she glanced at me and then added, "Those are the twins. They said they'd try to make it tonight but for sure will be here in the morning."

Wyatt tried again to speak but she went on. "Claire couldn't make it this year..."

"Second youngest," added Wyatt. "She's backpacking through Europe."

"And Vickie's around here somewhere. She was supposed to clean her room." She rolled her eyes. "Teenagers."

I giggled. My roommate at Juilliard was as messy as a teen.

Wyatt squeezed Anita's hand. "Ma, we can't stay. We're only here for a couple of hours and then have to get back on the road."

Anita studied his face for some time, maybe trying to find the joke in his eyes.

Just kidding, we're staying forever. Surprise!

"It's Christmas Eve, Wyatt. You're here now, the best Christmas present I could ask for...and you're not staying?" There was hurt in her voice and my heart cracked a little. I'd do anything to spend one more Christmas with *my* parents. I hardly knew my mother—what a gift Wyatt had.

"What about midnight Mass?" she asked. "It's a tradition."

Wyatt knit his brows together. I could tell he was conflicted. "Georgia's brother is getting married tomorrow and I promised I'd get her to L.A. on time."

Anita glanced at me, tears threatening at the rims of her eyes but she was trying hard not to show it. "A wedding on Christmas! That's wonderful." She stood, clearing her throat. "Then you really must go soon."

"We can stay for a little while, Ma. We've been driving for hours."

He had been driving for hours, not *we*. I abandoned my navigating duties in favor of a warm bed.

"Then you must be hungry," she replied with a brave smile. "I'll heat up some empanadas."

"We can stay," I blurted. Wyatt jerked his head toward me. "What time is your church service? Midnight? If we leave right afterward, we'll get to L.A. at eleven or so."

"I don't know." Wyatt shook his head. "That's cutting it awfully close."

"I told you the wedding's not until four. We'll totally make it. And you can take a nap."

Anita inclined her head in agreement. "She's got a point. You don't want to fall asleep on the road."

I silently congratulated myself for coming up with the plan.

"Okay," Wyatt agreed. "But only because I can't say no to two beautiful women."

Anita swatted him on the arm and scurried into the kitchen. Wyatt took my hand and whispered, "Thank you." His voice was a low rumble and made my insides melt. I breathed him in, so ready for a kiss. But then I remembered we were on his mother's couch and winked instead.

"De nada, limonada."

He arched a brow. "You speak Spanish?"

"No. I just memorize phrases I like. Do you? Your last name sounds Spanish. And your mom has an accent I can't place."

"That's the New Mexico accent. It's a mixture of Native American, Spanglish, and Southern, I guess."

"And Silva? Is that a Spanish name?"

"Portuguese, actually. Although my grandma used to say we were part Jewish and part Navajo." He shrugged one shoulder. "Then again, she also said she wrestled an alligator, so..."

I laughed. "Maybe she did."

"Maybe she *did*." He pulled me from the sofa and placed a warm hand on the small of my back. "I *do* know she had the best empanada recipe. My mom makes them every year."

My tummy growled in response. We hadn't had a good meal since the turkey.

"And a word of advice," he said as we walked. "Stay out of Vickie's room unless you want nightmares."

"I'll bear that in mind."

WYATT WASN'T KIDDING about the empanadas. They were sweet and savory at the same time, made with some kind of mincemeat, raisins, and pine nuts. The dough was a pillowy, deep-fried, out of body experience for my mouth. I ate five of them.

"This is the most amazing thing I've ever tasted," I said with a mouthful. I just couldn't get over it.

"It's the fresh-roasted piñóns from our orchard that make the difference," said Anita proudly.

"Were those all the trees I saw on the way in?"

"Piñón harvesting has been our family's livelihood since the eighteen-hundreds," said Wyatt.

I thought that was the coolest thing ever. Much cooler than my family's legacy as far as I was concerned. It seemed so rugged and earthy.

After we stuffed ourselves to the brim, Anita set some empanadas aside for our trip. Then, once Wyatt's phone charged for a little bit, I called Will. He barked at me for making him worry, then in a softer tone told me a friend of his could get a private plane ready in a matter of hours. He wasn't going to deal with any more of this road trip "nonsense."

Jaxson Knightly, an A-list director and one of my brother's groomsmen, had acquired his pilot's license and was poised to come rescue me.

"That's not scary at all," I half-joked. He didn't laugh.

In the end, I agreed to meet Jaxson at Santa Fe Regional Airport the next morning.

Anita was thrilled at the news and was already making plans to have an early morning gift exchange before we left. Wyatt questioned what we would do about the motor home. I suggested we could return to celebrate New Year's Eve with his family and drive back to California at a leisurely pace since the nuns didn't need it until January. I'd call and let them know. He brightened at the idea and was in the best of moods the rest of the evening.

Vicky came home. Finally. She was a sweet girl of seventeen. Not very talkative, but sweet.

Baking had always been a therapeutic pastime for me. It gave me a quiet outlet to spend time alone with clouds of flour and sugar. I loved making treats for my brother during the holidays and it did wonders to soften him up a bit when he was in a prickly mood. Sharing the baking experience with Wyatt's family gave me a sense of home I wasn't accustomed to. Anita and Vicky mixed the shortening, eggs, and anise seed while Wyatt and I measured the dry ingredients. Every so often his forearm would brush against mine alighting my skin with electricity. His lip curled ever so slightly and I knew he felt it, too. It became blatantly obvious he took advantage of the opportunity for little touches when he insisted on helping me roll out the dough.

Once the cookies were cooled and we'd finished them off with a dusting of cinnamon sugar, my senses were on overload. The scent of sweet anise filled the kitchen, spilling out into the living room and while we sampled our labors on the sofa, Wyatt's denim-clad leg intermittently bumped against my knee. I don't know which was more euphoric, the unbelievably delicious cookies or the exquisite delight of Wyatt's close proximity. Every bit of me was on fire—my blood intoxicated with overwhelming bliss.

I was grateful when Anita suggested we go into town early to reserve seats at the church and see the sights. The snowy streets of Santa Fe were exactly what I needed to cool down the fever in my beating pulse.

20

WYATT

Dad wasn't home when Georgia and I blew into town. If he knew we were coming, he might have blown off his domino game with his buddies, and he was near impossible to reach by cell phone. But at least he'd be at St. Francis Cathedral for Mass. Mom parked at the end of Canyon Road and said to meet at the Cathedral by eleven just in case we got separated.

"Your dad can't save seats once Lessons and Carols starts, so don't spend too much time fooling around." She stared directly at Vicky as she said this. My indifferent teenage sister glanced up from her phone long enough to pretend she was paying attention then went right back to her group chat.

"Lessons and Carols?" asked Georgia.

"The choir performs some music before church starts," I explained. "You'll like it, I think."

"You won't," chimed in Vicky, jumping out of the car. "Trust me."

So she *was* paying attention to the living after all.

"It's a little too archaic for her taste," I said, offering Georgia my hand. She smiled sweetly and pressed her delicate fingers in my palm. My heart sputtered to a stop. Her touch was that powerful.

"Archaic is right up my alley," she replied.

We made our way toward the park where we were to meet up with my sister Palanca, her husband Steven and little Sophia before trekking the mile or so on the Farolito Walk, ending at the Cathedral for midnight Mass. It was a family tradition, one I was anxious for Georgia to love as much as I did.

Her eyes lit with wonder when she saw the streets lined with thousands of candles.

"I've never seen so many luminaries," she exclaimed, pointing at the flickering lights in paper bags. "They make the snow look like it's glowing."

"Those aren't luminaries," Mom corrected gently, "Those are called farolitos. *Luminarias* are small bonfires...like that." She nodded toward the middle of the street where a small crowd formed, singing Christmas carols.

"Far-oh-lee-toes," Georgia intoned with a thumbs up. "Got it."

I snapped a photo, savoring the moment. The golden hue of the farolitos alighted the fringes of her honey locks fanning out from under her knit cap. Santa Fe agreed with her.

Mom spotted Palanca by the luminaria and ran to greet her, dragging Vicky along.

"I have to warn you about my sister," I said as we followed at a slow pace. "She's happily married and thinks everyone else should be too. She's gonna assume...ya know."

"That you brought a girl home to meet the family?"

"Yeah. So I apologize in advance."

Georgia gave me a side grin and fluttered her lashes. "I'm cool with that."

She brushed past me to introduce herself to my sister while I hung back with my jaw hinged open. Just as I suspected,

Palanca's eyes formed into giant wedding bells and looked from Georgia to me with a toothy grin. Steven welcomed Georgia with a friendly handshake and then she bent to greet Sophia in her umbrella stroller, bopping her on the nose.

Palanca formed an instant connection with Georgia and hooked arms with her as we began our trek down Canyon Road. Vicky found her teenage friends five minutes in and traveled the rest of the way in a giggling cluster. They were never too far away at any given moment and Mom kept a keen eye on Vicky even though they were good kids.

The Farolito Walk was every bit as magical as it was every year, but seeing it for the first time through Georgia's eyes gave me goose bumps. I snapped more candid shots of this small group of people I called my family—and of Georgia who fit in as though she'd always belonged. A pang shot in my heart—wanting her to feel the same but knowing after tomorrow, I might never see her again. Even our plans to return for the RV seemed too far-fetched. Her brother would never approve of me. I was fully prepared to make the trip solo.

We stopped at almost every house, gallery and shop along the way despite Mom's warnings earlier. She was the quintessential grandma, spoiling Sophia with candy and sweet sopapillas. In one of the shops she bought Sophia a plush Guadalupe doll and defended her purchase to Palanca by pointing out how Sophia should have something religious to occupy her little hands at church.

After that my sister put her foot down and banned Mom from any more stops. She hurried Mom along to the Cathedral claiming she was cold and tired and wanted a place to sit, and told Georgia and me to take our time.

"I'll let Sophia spread out across the pew," she said conspiratorially, "Just text me when you get there."

Alone at last. Or at least as alone as two people can be with hundreds of strangers around. The crowd had thinned out considerably by this time, most people enjoying the farolitos at dusk before heading to their Christmas Eve celebrations. Still, the street musicians were in full swing, playing their jazz Christmas songs and the hot chocolate carts were still out, offering free drinks to everyone. Georgia soaked up every sight, smell, and sound with awe, marveling at the spectacle around us.

"Do you have a gift for your mom?" she asked as we passed a small store.

"I, uh..." The truth was I had planned to pick something up for Mom in California after my gig. A sickly feeling clawed at my stomach. So much had changed and now there was no way I could crash the Darcy wedding for a cheap story. I had to find a way to tell Georgia the truth—preferably without her hating me for it.

"Come on." She tugged me inside the shop and we browsed for a while before she found a beaded chain of turquoise and coral. Mom would love it.

"Use the tip money," she said, and went off to window shop on her own. I took the opportunity to pick up a few other gifts, all the while wondering how I could tell Georgia my feelings. Hoping she felt it, too.

"I like your family," she said as we returned to the crisp night air, walking past the string of shops to a quieter portion of the road. We stopped to warm ourselves close to a crackling fire. "And you were right about your sister, Palanca. She reeeeally loves weddings."

"I'm so embarrassed." The last thing I needed was for my sister to scare Georgia away. I was perfectly capable of doing that myself.

"It's fine. She just wants to see you happy. I used to tease my brother all the time."

"I *am* happy," I said. "I'm like...the poster child for happy."

"Are you? Really?"

I met her gaze, studying her features in the flickering firelight. "I am now."

Her eyes flashed with awareness and she parted her lips ever so slightly before clearing her throat and turning her focus on the flames.

"Palanca said you've never brought a girl home to meet the family. Why's that?"

Wow. I was either going to squish a banana in Palanca's hair or send her a thank you card. Which one remained to be seen.

I let out a deep breath. "Because nobody ever mattered enough to me."

"No one?" She chuckled. "Not even evil rich girl?"

"Nobody," I whispered, nudging her chin toward me with my fingertip so I could fix my eyes on hers. "Until you."

I ran my thumb gently along her jaw, drawing myself closer. Her cheeks were warm from the fire yet I felt her shiver under my touch. Her breath hitched, a tiny sputtering of air catching in her chest. She was so incredibly lovely with her wide eyes and soft lips. A beautiful ache bloomed deep in my belly. I needed her. Not just physically. I needed her always and forever.

I searched her features, taking a snapshot of this moment. Burning it into my memory.

Then she grimaced, eyes rolling back and nostrils flaring. Was I off-putting? I made sure to brush my teeth before we left the house.

"What's wrong?" I asked, breaking the mood. "Are you okay?"

"I'm fine." She frowned. "Do I look that bad?"

"No," I blurted. "You don't look bad at all. You look...beautiful. I mean, you made a face and I thought maybe you were about to sneeze."

She blinked at me, confused. "That was my *kiss me now* face."

I stuttered, not certain I'd heard her correctly. "Y-y-you want me to..."

"Kiss me."

My heart leaped in my chest, galloping thunderously.

Yes, Ma'am!

I cradled the nape of her neck, angling her luminous face up to meet me and lowered my lips to hers. She sighed into the kiss —surrendering her whole being—breathing life into me.

An overwhelming desire came over me to protect her, cover her, shield her. Give her everything within my power to give.

My lips explored hers with slow, savoring caresses. Sweet. Gentle. She let out a little whimper. So responsive to my touch. I wrapped my arm around her waist and drew her to me, keeping her close to my chest. It's where I wanted her to live. Pressed against my heart for all eternity.

She slid her fingers under my coat, clinging to the fabric of my shirt. Delicious heat coursed through my veins, thick as molasses and I needed more of Georgia as a lifeline or my heart would certainly stop. I kissed her deeply, ardently, reverently. I felt her hand roam against my chest, passing my collar and through my hair. There, her delicate fingers traced the back of my neck sending delightful waves of electricity over my skin.

I was ready to declare my love right there and then.

Georgia was everything sweet and wonderful. Perfection. My joy was complete in her—a feeling so intense my heart cracked open. I could have danced and laughed and cried out in agony all at once. This feeling that could only be described as love was the most exquisite torture all summed up in a kiss.

The Cathedral bells chimed the half-hour, clanging loud

and strong. I softened my hold on Georgia and nipped her bottom lip once before breaking away. We rested our foreheads together and caught our breath, listening and waiting for the last bell to echo across the distance.

"Merry Christmas," I whispered, my voice a deep rumble. "Almost."

She smiled. "Merry Christmas."

The heat from the fire was delightful and cozy. I didn't want to walk away from our bubble of warmth but my family expected us to join them soon. I was tempted to text Palanca to tell her we would miss the service but Georgia tugged my arm and urged me to hurry. She didn't want to be late.

The church was incredibly beautiful, as it was every year. The Christmas trees inside were lit for the first time in the season indicating the end of Advent and the beginning of Christmastide. They were decorated simply with only white twinkle lights and nothing more. Candles and poinsettias adorned the altar and gold draperies were hung along the walls. It was a sight.

But it didn't compare to the fireworks going off in my heart. I was hyper aware of Georgia's presence beside me on the pew. Her face lit up from the moment the organ played the first note. She was enthralled with every aspect, especially the music. The choir sang majestically backed by a full orchestra for Handel's Messiah. Georgia's fingers played along on her lap, drumming out the piano part by memory. I rested my hand on my knee palm up—an invitation to quiet her nervous energy. She abandoned her air piano and knit her fingers through mine. An indescribable joy flooded my chest and a goofy grin spread across my cheeks, staying there all through the rest of the Mass. I was sure I frightened the priest when I went up for communion.

The sappy, ridiculous expression remained plastered on my

face until we returned to the house. Vicky's the one who pointed it out to me.

"What's wrong with you, weirdo?" She rolled her eyes. "Never mind. I don't want to know." Then she shuffled off to bed. Reeses greeted us as soon as we walked in, bouncing at our feet, frantically wagging his tail. I scooped him up and scratched behind his ears to make up for leaving him behind.

Dad was impressed with Georgia. Then again she was the embodiment of charm and had Dad eating out of the palm of her hand with just one kiss to the cheek. He winked at me and mouthed *She's a keeper*.

Palanca retired to her old room with Sophia, who'd zonked out in the car on the way home. She was too young to understand the whole Santa thing. Next year she'd be hard to get to sleep.

Mom prepared the trundle in Vicky's room for Georgia and warned us not to stay up too late before leaving us alone. Georgia and I sat by the fireplace after everyone had gone to sleep, listening to Christmas music at a low volume. I knew we had an early start in the morning, but I couldn't tear myself away from her. She was effervescent in the glow of the crackling fire and the red chili pepper lights on our tree. It was good to be home for Christmas. And with Georgia, it was the most perfect Christmas I could hope for.

We curled on the sofa watching the fire dance to the soft music, whispering to one another and laughing at all our adventures. Every time she smiled I captured her mouth, pressing her lips with sweet kisses. She was *the one*. I was certain of it, more than I had ever been sure of anything in my life. It took every ounce of willpower not to blurt *I love you* in between kisses. That would scare her off for sure.

We spent long moments just studying each other's features. She caressed her fingers along my forearm. I twisted a lock of her soft hair. Her gaze drifted along every inch of my face, watching me. There was a whole world in her eyes. Would I find a place for me in there?

"I want to give you your present now," I said, reaching for one of my shopping bags. "I didn't have time to wrap it."

Georgia furrowed her brows. "I didn't get you anything."

"Yes you did." I kissed her. "You gave me a Christmas Miracle."

She snorted and nudged my knee. "You know what I mean."

"It's just a little trinket. You're gonna laugh. Here."

She took the present and felt for the contents inside. Her fingers squeezed at the cardboard box through the paper bag as if she could take a guess what it might be then shook it by her ear.

"I think you'll be disappointed after all this hype. Open it."

She smirked at me and ripped the bag to shreds, crumpled it up in a ball and threw it at me. Then her eyes grew wide when she saw the box.

"I love it," she gasped, tearing open the lid. She took the gift from the box and unwrapped it from the plastic. "It's so cute."

It was pretty nice, actually. I wasn't sure what the miniature replica of Charlie Brown's Christmas tree would look like out of the package considering it was roughly the size of a teacup, but I was pleasantly surprised at the detail. It was supposed to be a gag gift, but Georgia's reaction was priceless. She kissed me over and over again.

"Thank you, Charlie Brown." Her smile was radiant. "It's perfect."

She was perfect.

We were roused by the jazzy orchestrations of *The Christmas Song* by Nat King Cole. No Christmas was complete without the soothing, mellow timbre of his voice.

"I love this song," Georgia said with a sigh.

"Me too." I slipped off the couch and offered her my hand. "Care to dance?"

She snickered. "How can I be sure it won't end with you crashing into the Christmas tree?"

"Just hold me tight."

I pulled her into my arms and we swayed to the music. Her body was soft pressed against mine. She fused into me, filling all the gaps between us.

My heart swelled along with the music, so full and so happy. I pressed my lips to her forehead, trailing butterfly kisses along her temple, and down her jawbone. My mouth lingered near her ear, dying to tell her my feelings.

"Georgia..." I breathed, my heart pounding so hard it hurt. She shifted just enough to focus on my face. Her expression spoke to me. Trusting.

Tell me. Say anything.

I brushed a stray tendril from her shoulder and leveled my gaze on her eyes.

"I think I'm falling in love with you."

She arched a brow, reflecting on my admission. "Think?"

I paused before admitting, "No. Not think. I know I am."

She started giggling. Really tittering to herself.

"I'm glad you find that amusing," I deadpanned. "For my next act—"

Her lips crashed onto mine, shutting me up. She laughed into the kiss. I was a goner. She could laugh at me all she wanted for all I cared, as long as she kissed me like this every day.

"Thank you for saying it first. I thought I was being a silly girl, falling in love so quickly."

I blinked in astonishment. "You love me?"

She bobbed her head, eyes wide. "It's crazy, right?"

"Not as crazy as living life without you."

We gazed lovingly into each other's eyes for exactly two seconds and then cracked up. It was all so wild.

"Too sappy?"

She threw her arms around my neck. "I like your brand of sappy."

We danced to the end of the song and then danced some more. It was all out in the open now. I could breathe freely.

A throat cleared behind us. It was Steven tiptoeing into the living room. "Sorry to barge in. Palanca put me on Santa duty."

"No worries," Georgia chirped. "Tell us what to do. We'll be your elves."

He rubbed his eyes, too tired to protest. "I was just going to put out milk and cookies."

"We got this." I nudged him back down the hallway. "We'll even take a few bites to make it realistic."

"Are you sure?" He looked over his shoulder to Georgia.

"Yes," I said. "Go to sleep."

He shuffled off, waving tiredly. Once he was gone I inclined my head to the kitchen. "Let's go get those cookies."

Georgia started, then stopped when my phone buzzed on the side table. "Who's texting at two in the morning?"

I shrugged. "Maybe it's your brother. I'll go get the cookies while you check."

I pranced into the kitchen and Reeses perked his head from his slumber with the hope of food.

"Are you hungry buddy?"

He trotted to the refrigerator and scratched the door.

"You know where the good stuff is, don't you? Let's see what we've got."

I found some lunchmeat and tossed him a slice. Then I eyed the carrots and thought it would be fun to leave those out for the reindeer. Sophia would get a kick out of that.

I wondered if Georgia wanted kids someday. My heart

warmed at the thought, hoping to be the one she'd share that joy with. How long would I have to wait to ask her to marry me? Was right now too soon? Yeah, maybe just a tad. Tomorrow, then. I grinned, almost talking myself into it.

Once I gathered the milk, cookies, and carrots on a tray, I shut off the kitchen light and strolled back to the living room. But I stopped short as I crossed the threshold when I saw Georgia standing in the middle of the room with the phone hanging at her side and tears streaming down her cheeks.

21

GEORGIA

I had to squint through the massively cracked screen on Wyatt's phone to make sure I was reading the text correctly.

Will Darcy wedding...

At first I thought it was my brother being weird, talking about himself in third person. Or maybe Stella or somebody with a droll sense of humor hijacked his phone.

Ha ha. Got your brother's phone.

Like he was a toddler and they were pretending to catch his nose but it was their thumb all along. I dunno. It was two in the morning and I had just been kissed like there was no tomorrow. I was kinda loopy.

But then I realized, through the copious amounts of cracks (seriously, how did he deal with that phone?) that the texts were from some guy named T Dawg. I scrolled, just to be sure, and that's when I found the long string of texts from this T Dawg guy about my brother. More specifically, my brother's wedding to Beth and the vendor pass he acquired for Wyatt for his exposé story.

My heart dropped to my navel with a definitive thump. The top-secret news story Wyatt was looking forward to. It was about my brother. And not in a good way. What sort of gossip did he think he would uncover? Since Will met Beth, he became even more boring than he was before. All sappy lovey dovey *let's stay in and cuddle tonight* kind of boring. Nobody was cheating. Beth wasn't prego. Not a gold digger in sight. There was literally no dirt a slimy gossip writer could dig up on my brother and his bride. Slimy being the operative word here. I felt slimy. Or rather...slimed on. Wyatt was just another guy using me to get to my brother. And I fell fast and hard. Stupid me.

I felt numb all over. I didn't even notice I was crying until my eyes puffed up so much I couldn't see straight. Wyatt was just a blurry form to me as he came into the living room. All I could make out through my foggy vision was this blob of a man bouncing in all jolly and clueless then freezing at the doorway.

Jig's up, blockhead. I can see right through that adorably klutzy facade.

"Georgia...are you okay?" asked the traitor. "What happened?"

"What happened?" I spat. "I fell for your...your...deception. That's what happened." I wagged the phone around. "Who's T Dawg?"

Understanding dawned on his face—at least what I could see of his face through the rainstorm in my eyes. I wiped them with the heel of my thumb so I could see better. See the disappointment in Wyatt's silly and annoyingly handsome face.

He took a step toward me. "I can explain—"

"Don't come any closer."

He paused, looked at the tray, twisted left and right, then resolved to set the tray on the floor for lack of a nearby table. I just stood there waiting to see what kind of two-faced, phony, rascally explanation he would come up with. He raked his hands through is stupidly beautiful hair.

"I was going to tell you."

"Oh? When, pray tell? Or were you too busy lying to me? Telling me you *luuurve* me."

"I do love you."

"Stop. Just stop." I tossed him the phone. It slipped through his fingers and landed at his feet. He didn't make a move to pick it up. "Just tell me something that isn't a lie."

He exhaled a heavy sigh and squeezed his temple. "Alright. T Dawg is one of my old roommates who moved to L.A. and now works at some catering place."

"The wedding caterer?"

"Yeah. The thing is, I still owe him some rent money and when he caught wind of this wedding, he thought we could both cash in."

"That's an asinine idea," I snapped.

"I see that now. But I promise you—I'm not going to go through with it."

I huffed. "Of course not. You won't get anywhere near my house."

"Georgia, please..."

"You know what?" I hissed. "As angry as I am with you, and believe me I'm raging mad, I blame myself. I let you in. Exposed my heart. And that just makes me really freaking sad."

I couldn't speak any more. The tears were burning my throat. Wyatt just stared at me. A deer in the headlights.

"Goodbye, Wyatt." I turned on my heel, puffed up my chest, and strode across the living room out the front door. It was one of those *these boots are made for walkin'* moments. I was empowered.

I will survive, suckah!

Until the arctic blast attacked me and I noted the flaw in my dramatic exodus. I left my coat inside. Also, I had no idea how to drive that RV so I scurried back into the warm house. Wyatt was still standing there with the tray at his feet except now Reeses was digging into the cookies.

I raised my chin, trying to play it cool. "I have decided to leave first thing in the morning."

I began toward Vicky's room, forced to pass Wyatt on the way. He stopped me with a light touch on my arm.

"Can we discuss this in the morning?" he begged.

I shrugged him off. "We'll see."

I gave Reeses one hearty scratch and went to bed. Not that I slept at all. Around four thirty in the morning, *sooo* over the tossing and turning, I gathered my things (which consisted of my coat and the empanadas Anita packed for me) and paced the living room. Maybe I'd call an Uber? I had no plan. I only knew I had to be gone before Wyatt woke up.

"You still up?"

I turned to see Steven shuffling over, scratching his bed head and yawning as he spoke. His eyes weren't completely open, either.

"Actually," I admitted, my throat thick with tears, "I need to go. Do you think I could use the phone to call a taxi?"

He blinked at me, clearing the sleep from his eyes, then furrowed his brows when he saw the state I was in.

"Are you okay?" He looked around. "Where's Wyatt?"

I shook my head, willing the tears away. "I just need to go home."

The head shaking didn't work. Thunderstorms flooded from my tear ducts.

"Okay, okay." Steven sprang into crisis responder mode. Husbands with babies were good at that sort of thing. "Where's home? How can I help?"

Awww. What a guy.

"I have a plane to catch," I sobbed. "Santa Fe airport."

He held up a finger. "Let me just get my keys."

And just like that, this nice man who hardly knew me took me to the airport. No questions asked. Surely he didn't want to hear how much of a scoundrel his brother-in-law was. It wasn't my place to expect him to. Here we were on Christmas Day, the sun just a flicker on the horizon. He could have been cozy and warm, waiting to capture his daughter's reaction on camera when she found her presents. But something in his weary expression showed a genuine concern.

"Are you going to be okay? I could park and walk you in."

We were idling at the drop off curb. The airport was so tiny and empty I imagined he could leave the car there and nobody would complain. But I didn't want to keep him from his family.

"No, I'm good." I attempted a smile. "Thanks for the ride."

I reached for the door handle to get out of the car.

"Listen," he said, gently bidding me to wait. "I don't know what happened between you and my brother-in-law—and it's none of my business. I'm sure you have a valid reason for leaving. But just so you know...Wyatt's a straight up guy. He might be a wayward clown. A little lost sometimes. Actually he's kind of a yo-yo."

"I'm...not sure where you're going with this."

"The point is, whatever dorky thing he might have done, that man is in love with you. It's all over his face. I've never seen him like that."

He shrugged, having fulfilled his obligatory brother-in-law endorsement.

I gave him a half-smile. "Merry Christmas."

"Merry Christmas," he replied. "Have a safe flight."

Minutes later I was inside the terminal wondering what I'd do to pass the few extra hours besides feel sorry for myself. Jaxson wasn't due to arrive for a while and even though I was hurt and mad, a small part of me was hoping for a grand gesture from Wyatt. One of those airport scenes in every rom-com where the guy crashes through security to stop the girl from boarding a plane. But Wyatt was probably still sleeping.

Turned out, I didn't have to wait at all. It was the Australian accent that caught my attention. I spotted Jaxson Knightly chatting it up with one of the aforementioned security guards. Probably the only security guard in this cute little airport. They'd gotten coffee from somewhere. I clutched my little bag of empanadas. Would it be worth it to trade one for a cup of joe? Nah.

"How are you here so early?" I asked Jaxson after we said our hellos.

The security guard had to get back to work and tipped his baseball cap to me. Jaxson clapped him on the shoulder. "See ya around, mate."

That Jaxson. Made friends everywhere he went. He smiled at me. "You want to know why I arrived so early. Well, the truth is, I've never flown such a distance in one go. So I erred on the side of caution."

"You are not making me feel overly confident to get in a plane with you."

He laughed, a deep rumble comforting my scuffed up heart. "It's perfectly safe. Ready to go?"

"Yeah."

If he was wondering where my traveling companion was, he didn't show it. He escorted me to his plane, all fueled up and waiting for us. We slipped on our headsets and once we got the A-OK from the control tower and ran all the checks, we were on our way. My stomach flipped at first, but I soon got used to the sensation of flying in a tiny aircraft. Jaxson maneuvered like a pro—he even looked the part of a G.A. pilot with his leather jacket and aviators.

"Thank you for coming all this way to get me," I said into the headset. It really was too kind of him to leave his wife on Christmas morning. They were still technically newlyweds. "My brother said Emma might come with to keep you company."

"She wanted to come," he replied. "But she's in no condition to fly."

"Oh no. Is something wrong?"

A huge grin split his face. "Everything's perfect."

Oh. OH! He meant...wow. Emma Woods expecting. My thoughts turned to Wyatt, how Emma was his celebrity crush. How I secretly wished he were here. Then I kicked that thought to the curb. No. I slapped it across the face, beat it to a pulp, *and then* kicked it to the curb. Take *that*, sentimental feelings.

"Congratulations," I said. "That's great news."

"Thanks. We're still keeping it close to our chest, though."

We buzzed along through the sky with the sun at our backs. The sights down below were stunning. The rocky terrain of the desert coming to life in hues of pink and purple. It was almost cathartic.

I wondered what Wyatt was doing just then. Would he just be waking up? How long before he noticed I was gone? Would he go outside to see the sunrise on his beautiful pine nut orchard?

Annoyed with my pestering thoughts, I shoved my hands in my coat pockets. One of them had something pokey inside. My hand dug it out and I was sad all over again. The miniature Charlie Brown Christmas tree. I thought I'd left it behind. Wyatt must have tucked it in my pocket after our fight.

I ran a finger over the tiny plastic pine needles and the little scrap of blue felt serving as Linus' blanket. My heart ripped open anew with the memories contained in that silly tree. How Wyatt kissed me and told me he loved me. It didn't seem like he was lying at the time. Steven's parting words still echoed around in my brain. *That man is in love with you.*

Tears burnt the edges of my eyes. Maybe there was some truth to that. Wyatt's kisses were certainly convincing enough. It didn't matter, though. It was over. And now I would never watch Peanuts the same way again.

22

GEORGIA

I hugged my brother long and hard. A death grip, really. Which only set off alarm bells in his overactive imagination.

"What's going on, George? Is it the guy? What did he do to you?"

"Sheesh! Can't a girl hug her brother on his wedding day? These are tears of joy."

He wasn't buying it. He gave me a long hard look.

"It's fine, really," I said. "He decided to stay with his family for Christmas, that's all."

"And you miss him?"

I spat though my lips. "Ha! Of course not. I don't even know the guy." I forced a fake, maniacal laugh. He arched a brow. There was a reason he was the actor in the family and not me.

"Then why is your face all blotchy?"

"Gee, thanks."

He scowled. "We could teach him a lesson. I know a guy."

"Whaaat? No. Besides, you don't know a guy. Big fat liar."

"Seth. He'd do it." He paced, rubbing his chin. Was he a crime boss all of a sudden? I go away for a *few months!*

"Seth? The guy who played Large Larry in that one movie? He's a big teddy bear."

"It's called acting. If he's convincing enough, Ice Boy will wet his pants and run for the hills. Seth is definitely our guy."

Will took to calling Wyatt *Ice Boy* after the rental car incident. I didn't bother correcting him.

"Um...aaaanyway. No need to send your actor friends on my behalf. There's nothing going on. *You* just concentrate on getting married." I rocked my fists in the air. "Yay!"

I checked in on Beth next because —*obvs*—she wasn't allowed in the same room as Will. Bad luck and all that. Her bestie Jane was with her. They were getting the spa treatment and couldn't move from their lounging chairs without dripping whatever goop was on their faces.

"Come join us," chirped Beth. "We reserved a place for you."

"No thanks." I thumbed over my shoulder. "Gotta go wrap all my Amazon deliveries. Boy, did they pile up."

Jane took a hold of my hand and craned her eyes to see me. "Please stay. It won't be the same without you."

That was the thing about Jane. Too sweet for words and who could resist?

"Okay."

The truth was, I probably needed it after the workout my puffy eyes had gone through. Beth called in the professional beautician they'd contracted for the day. Will's idea, not hers. Then the lady spread a green paste all over my face and left me there to sprout. It was equal parts creepy crawly and soothing.

Beth and Jane asked me all sorts of questions. Mostly about Wyatt. No doubt she'd been talking to Will.

"We were worried about you when you left that message you'd been robbed," she said.

I apologized for causing them alarm.

Then she said, "We almost postponed the wedding."

That would have been like a sad sit com. *Little Georgia Ruins Things* take two. Cue the laugh track.

"Well, I'm glad you didn't. The show must go on."

Beth and Jane laughed at my lame attempt at a joke. They were both theatre people so they appreciated showbiz humor. Actually, lots of Beth's theatre friends were coming to the wedding. Her old roommate, Lydia, who I'd heard so much about. I was looking forward to meeting her. There were also some other girls from when Beth and Will performed *Pirates of Penzance* together. Then of course there was Stella. She claimed she was responsible for the wedding with her mad matchmaking skills. Nobody argued with her because she was knighted by the Queen and all.

When I was done growing a small garden on my face I took to my room to have some alone time. Big mistake. All I did was pine over Wyatt. No pun intended. I lost track of time after my shower—just sitting on my bed wrapped in a towel. Staring at the Charlie Brown tree.

Stella came in looking all regal and proper. All she needed was a fascinator to complete the ensemble. She sat next to me on the bed and talked about everything *except* my wacky road trip. That was a relief.

Then she did what Stella does best—dole out cryptic words of wisdom.

"Do you know what I find fascinating?" she said.

"The tiny legs on Yorkies?"

"How Beth was ready to see the worst in your brother based on half-truths. Imagine if she never listened to his side of the story. If she would have continued to misjudge him we wouldn't be celebrating a wedding here today. Imagine that."

"Yeah. Imagine that."

She voiced a sigh like a deflated siren. "I think about these things from time to time. Don't you?"

"No. Not really."

She held out her hand for the tree I was twiddling. "May I?"

"Sure." I handed it over.

"Ah. I really like this movie." She examined it closely, turning it over in her hand. "Those children judged that poor little tree. But in the end all it needed was some love from a boy and his dog."

She gave it back and I marveled at it like she'd performed some kind of magic. But it was just the same old bric-a-brac.

"Well poppet, I best be going before I miss the whole wedding. And you might want to put on some clothes so you can perform your bridesmaid duties. Your future sister-in-law is waiting for you."

Then she took off, leaving me with that little nugget. A boy and his dog indeed.

IT DOESN'T GET MUCH BETTER than a sunset wedding. Especially on Christmas. The guest list was relatively small so there was plenty of room for the ceremony on the terrace overlooking the lawns of Pemberley. I'd always enjoyed the view from this part of the house where I could look down on the neighborhood like a queen on a hill. On a clear day you could see the Hollywood sign.

A dozen or so Christmas trees served as decorations along the rows of chairs and a canopy of white lights was strung above our heads. It was like a fairy tale.

We lined up to go out by the glass doors. Beth held on to her father's arm while Jane fluffed the wedding dress. Lady, our Cocker Spaniel, was the ring bearer. Just fake rings, though. My brother was in place where the groom is supposed to go. A little fidgety. Stern face. There was his best friend, Bing, at his side, anxiously waiting for the women to emerge—particularly Jane. We were all wondering when *that* wedding would occur. Bing proposed to Jane a year ago.

The quartet of musicians began playing *Oh What A Circus* from *Evita*. (Don't ask.) Then the wedding coordinator ushered us out. I never knew where to cast my eyes while walking down the aisle. Same thing happened when I was a bridesmaid for my friend Lisa. At least the bride could look at the groom. I didn't have that. I couldn't very well look at the minister. Awkward. If I looked left and right, smiling at the wedding guests, I'd be tempted to do the windshield wiper princess wave. *Wipe, wipe, wipe...show off the dirt.*

Beth's little sister Mary went before me. She was too busy concentrating on her feet. Step, touch. Step, touch. Yeeeah. I wasn't going to do that. No way. I decided I'd act all casual.

Just taking a stroll on the veranda. With a bouquet of flowers. La ti da.

I focused on the view beyond the terrace. The hill leading up to our property. It was a beautiful, clear evening. A little chilly for California, but after getting stranded in Nebraska, this was balmy. I winked at Will the last second before taking my spot next to Mary. That relaxed his face a bit. I almost got a smile out of him. Then the music swelled, Beth appeared looking radiant, and my brother's face morphed into sunshine incarnate.

It was a special day. I wanted to soak it all up and tuck these little moments in my memories. For my sake and for my parents. I imagined they were there in spirit. The minister began his dearly beloved speech. Beth's dad handed her off to Will with a handshake. Her mom cried.

I was really trying to pay attention to the ceremony without letting my mind wander to thoughts of Wyatt. What was wrong with me? It was one of my family's most important life events and here I was throwing myself a pity party. I looked out across the vast lawns of Pemberley for just a second. The security detail were up to something. Congregating with their golf carts. I focused back on the wedding. Bing was digging in his pocket for the rings. A few people chuckled when he pretended he lost them. Lady gently tapped at his pant leg with her furry paw. Everyone awwwwed.

I caught more movement in the corner of my eye. The security guys again, moving around excitedly. They looked like little plastic figurines from where I stood.

Will and Beth had the rings now, ready to slide them on each other's fingers. My brother was all smiles and sappy eyes.

Beth, it is with all my love that I give you this ring...

Muffled shouts echoed from down below. The guys were yelling at someone. I couldn't see past where the driveway curved down the hill, but just behind the trees, I thought I made out the outline of a Winnebago. *The* Winnebago. The security guards rushed behind the trees. I craned my neck but lost sight of them. Then, a figure of a man emerged on the roof of the motor home, waving frantically with both arms. Wyatt. Was he still trying to get his story? He was shouting something at the house.

I take you for now and for always...

One of the security guards was on the roof of the RV now, trying to coax Wyatt down. That made Wyatt wave his arms more desperately, jumping up and down. He shouted louder. It sounded like my name.

"Georgia! Georgia!"

Oh, my goodness. *This* was his grand gesture? Here. At my brother's wedding. On a Winnebago. My mouth hinged open and I glanced back at my brother to see if he'd noticed the commotion going on. He was too focused on Beth. I tried to casually slice my hand across my throat in the universal gesture to cut it out. Wyatt was too far away to see. I motioned a little bigger. Then bigger until my arm flew in a grand swiping motion, almost smacking Mary in the face. The security guy had Wyatt in a police hold, hands behind his back.

"Georgia!" he cried even louder than before. "I looove you!"

I felt a hundred eyeballs on me as I watched the guard shuffle Wyatt off. I glanced over to see Will glaring down at the lawns, stormy eyes a fierce blue. Then he turned to me and said, "Is that Ice Boy?"

I nodded, red-faced with mortification. *Little Georgia Ruins Things* take three.

Clap.

Will ticked his head at Ephraim, our groundskeeper, (who over the years had become more like a cousin we pay to do things) and in a flash he slipped down the back staircase. When I looked back to find Wyatt, all I saw were a couple of golf carts driving back toward the house.

Will cleared his throat. "Shall we continue?"

The minister straightened and humorously addressed the wedding guests, "This is why I never ask if anyone objects."

That earned him a few giggles. Then he pronounced the couple man and wife. They kissed, everyone applauded, and the Wyatt fiasco was quickly forgotten. By most everyone except me—and Stella—who arched a severe eyebrow at me.

As soon as we processed down the aisle and through the glass doors, Beth took me by the hand, stared squarely in my eyes, and said, "Go."

"I'm sorry I ruined your wedding," I sobbed.

"You didn't ruin anything. Now go get your man."

I turned my gaze to my brother expecting to see his stern

frowny face. But he smiled softly and nodded, agreeing with his wife.

His wife. Gah! So cool.

I gave them both air kisses and took off in search of Wyatt. The RV was still parked on the grounds but I couldn't find the security team. I went around the house, looking outside and inside with no luck. Where in Pemberley would they have taken him? It's not like we had a dungeon for intruders. Those guys were just a security service my brother hired out when he had special events. They had limited access.

I was about ready to scream in frustration when I heard a *pssst*. It was Ephraim at the other end of a hallway. He motioned me over.

"There's a guy in the media room who wants to talk to you. He seems a little loco, ya know what I mean?"

"It's okay. You go enjoy the wedding. I'll take it from here."

He smirked and trotted back upstairs.

The media room, as my brother liked to call it, was actually a small movie theater with luxury seating. There was even a small concession area in the entryway. I found Wyatt fiddling with the controls on one of the chairs raising and lowering his feet. He jumped up when he saw me enter, taking me in with wide eyes.

"Wow."

I wanted to fly to his arms. He was grubby looking but I'd missed him. My heart hurt so much. But I wouldn't be the fool. I wouldn't let my love for him cloud my judgment. I had to know first if he was here for me or his story. I crossed my arms, mostly to keep them from curling around his waist to squeeze him into me.

He reached his hands out pleadingly. "Before you throw me out or send me to the tower to be executed, hear me out."

He sighed, seemingly at a loss for words. Then he said, "I

had a long drive to think about what I'd say. Grovel. Beg. Try to explain my stupidity. But now—seeing you here—I realize my words are small. Who am I? Nobody."

I wanted to interrupt him to say he wasn't a nobody to me. He looked so pathetic, though. Like a sad, hungry puppy. I remained quiet so he could finish his speech.

"I don't deserve you," he said after a pause. "Not even close. But I promise, if you give me a chance, I'll do anything—work my tail off—to deserve your love and forgiveness someday."

My heart soared. But I didn't betray that in my face. I recalled what Stella said earlier. How Beth changed her mind about my brother after he told his side of the story. This was Wyatt's chance to do the same.

"What about your article?" I asked tentatively.

"I don't care about any of that. I don't think I ever did."

His eyes searched mine. Looking for a sliver of hope.

"That was some scene you made."

He grimaced. "I had to get in here somehow."

"Oh? Didn't you have a vendor pass from...T Dawg?" Ugh. It embarrassed me just to use the word *T Dawg* in a sentence.

"No. I made an anonymous call to the caterer because I suspected T Dawg was selling vendor passes."

"Really?"

"Yeah. He sort of let it slip when I phoned him to call off our deal this morning. But that meant my pass no longer worked." He shrugged. "I guess I shot myself in the foot."

A sentimental lump swelled in my throat. "You called off the deal?"

"Georgia..." He moved to me, closing the gap between us. I could feel the warmth of his presence. "I should have called it off a lot sooner." He took my hand. "I'm sorry I ever got involved in that whole thing."

He was trembling, his breath an anxious quiver as he

watched me with imploring eyes. So close. Drawing me in like the center of gravity.

"I'm not," I replied.

His eyes widened just a little. "You're not?"

"No. Because I would have never met you otherwise." I raised myself on my tippy toes so our noses touched. When I spoke, my lips moved over his in a breathy whisper. "You're my Christmas miracle."

He captured my mouth, kissing me with every ounce of his soul. Filling me up. Completing me. My heart squeezed. I loved this hot mess of a guy.

He sucked in a deep breath and wrapped me in the most perfect hug. His heart pounded against my ear. I could have stayed like that forever if I didn't want to kiss him again so badly.

He trailed a gentle touch over my hair and backed away to cup my face, pressing his lips on mine with several tiny kisses in a row. Then he smiled and gazed in my eyes with quiet wonder.

"I love you, Miss Darcy," he said, his voice a soft rumble. "I know I must drive you crazy…"

"You can drive me anywhere," I said, shushing him with a finger on his lips. "Even crazy in love."

EPILOGUE - 4 YEARS LATER
WYATT

UNTYING the string of my custom made apron, I squeezed JoAnne in a hug. She'd been my gravy partner for five Christmases in a row and presented me with the handmade creation this morning.

"For the best mashed potato server this side of Kansas," she'd said with a proud grin. She had mad embroidery skills and stitched an image of Reeses with a Santa hat on the front. The caption said *Feliz Navidog*.

"Another successful year in the books," I said. After five Christmases serving turkey dinner at Hope Church she and I were the dynamic duo of mashed spuds and gravy. Even though I had my eye on the carving job I didn't think I could part with JoAnne. Not like Ralph would ever give up his spot.

"Will I see you and Georgia at the cafe tonight?" she asked. "I'll help out with the children as long as you two sing your famous duet."

"We wouldn't dare miss it," I said. "It's a tradition."

I kissed her cheek and made myself a small plate before the Living Nativity got started. Man, those mashed potatoes were good. A.J. really raised the culinary bar since he was allowed in the kitchen for the first time this year. The kid was going places.

Teresa found me, glancing at her watch. "There you are. Ready to get into costume?"

"Yup." I shoveled the last bite into my mouth and tossed the plate in the trash. "Where's Georgia?"

"Last time I checked Joy was helping her get ready. I think they're in places by now."

Joy was home from college for winter break and had been a big help to Georgia and me.

I thanked Teresa and hurried over to the makeshift dressing rooms. Once I slipped on my robes I went to take my place in the manger scene. Georgia was there already and when I saw her my heart sputtered to a stop. She always stirred little explosions in my chest, but tonight she was exceptionally radiant. Maybe it was the way the warm lights shone on her, casting soft shadows in the folds of her garments. Maybe it was the cream-colored robes with hints of blue stitched in. Maybe it was seeing her with our newborn son in her arms, cradling him gently and lovingly.

Joy was dressed as a shepherd's wife and it was her duty to keep our two-year old toddler, Noel, from getting into things. So far she was only somewhat successful. Noel already had her sticky candy cane full of hay.

"Look at that," I said with exaggerated interest. "What is it?"

"Nudding."

"Nothing? Can Daddy have it?" I glanced over at Georgia and winked. She watched with amusement.

Noel vehemently shook her head. "No."

"Not even if we trade?" I fished a small plush sheep from the deep pockets of my robes. Noel's eyes lit up and she happily made the trade.

I held the offending candy cane up for Georgia to examine. "Mary, did you know?"

She rolled her eyes. "I have no idea where she got that."

"My fault," Joy admitted. "I didn't think she actually knew how to open the plastic wrap."

Georgia and I both laughed. Noel could get into anything if she set her mind to it. We hardly ever gave her sweets but her birthday was Christmas Eve so we let it slide.

I squatted next to Georgia, first kissing little Wolfgang on the head and then my wife on her sweet lips.

"This is a good look on you," I said between kisses. "And you say you're not an actress."

"One night only," she joked. "Special engagement."

I raised one brow and clicked my tongue. "Hmmm. I don't think so. You need to beat Suzy McCormick's record."

She choked on a laugh. "Ten kids? Dream on."

"Six, then."

We'd talked about having a big family when we were first

married. But even then she didn't think I was serious about it. Oh but I was so, so serious.

She snorted and shook her head. I'd have to use my persuasive techniques later on.

A moment later, Reeses came bounding up into the manger scene dressed as a sheep. One of the ladies in the knitting ministry made him a little costume so he could join us. I had a feeling he'd steal the show. A.J. followed behind with the leash, rolling it up to hide it behind a rock. This year he was promoted to shepherd boy. His grandmother couldn't be prouder. Lois came along with a camera, clicking away before we were all in our positions.

"Just taking behind-the-scenes candids," she said.

A.J. scooped Reeses in his arms and posed. He didn't get the whole candid shot idea. They were quite a pair.

We were roused from the photo shoot to the sound of the megaphone announcement coming down the path.

"Five minutes," Pastor Kevin repeated at every group until he reached us. He climbed up to clap me on the back. "You ready, Joseph?"

"I was born for this role," I replied with a wink.

He grinned. "Oh, and thanks for donating the heat packs. I always wondered how they filmed those snow scenes in the movies without freezing their tails off."

I'd acquired the heat pads from the studio that picked up my latest spec script. I'd sold a couple of screenplays over the last few years, but my main gig was writing for a sit-com. One of these days, once I had more clout in the biz, I wanted to write an epic Sci-Fi flick for my brother-in-law.

Sisters Edna and Patty stopped by to tell us *break-a-leg*, and before Kevin ushered them inside for the start of the show, he led us all in a prayer.

My heart swelled. I knew Georgia and I would have our

large family someday, no matter how many children we were blessed with. These people in the little town of Bethlehem were, in many ways, family to us. It was our second home for several months of the year. A few weeks in summer, some time in the spring, but always at Christmas.

I watched Georgia with her angelic glow, smiling into the distance.

"You just had a happy thought," I observed.

She hitched one shoulder. "I have an idea for your next screenplay," she said. "It should involve a grounded plane, an unplanned road trip, and a dog."

"Oh? Is it a romance?"

She beamed. "Most definitely."

"Yeah. I think you're onto something. It could have some adventure, too. The hero's got to be a real stud muffin." I stroked my scruffy whiskers. "I'm thinking Henry Cavill or The Rock."

She gave me a saucy look. "Or...and I'm just brainstorming here...he could be nerdy and klutzy and endearing."

I tapped my chin, pretending to really think about it. "Hmmm. Do you think our heroine would fall for a guy like that?"

"She'd fall, alright. Right over his dog. Then she'd keep falling until she was completely, perfectly, and incandescently in love."

A sweet warmth filled my chest. "And how does the movie end?"

Wolfgang squirmed in her arms on the verge of waking and Georgia rocked him softly back into dreamland. She swaddled him in his blankets a little more snugly and kissed his head.

"The ending is easy," she said with a lovely smile. "They live happily ever after."

"Yes," I agreed, glancing at Noel who was occupied with her

stuffed animal, then back to my beautiful wife. "It's perfect. They all live happily ever after."

WHAT TO READ NEXT
Backstage Romance continues in:

THE FRIEND ACT

Best friends don't kiss. But under the stage lights, all bets are off.

It's all an act and I don't care. When it comes to Edmund Bertram I'll take what I can get.

Yes, THE Edmund Bertram.

YouTube star and all-around popular guy, Edmund Bertram. He also happens to be my childhood BFF.

Can I convince him the love I declare for him on stage is real, or will he think it's all a song and dance?

GET THE FRIEND ACT HERE

Join me every Sunday for my ridiculous Newsletter tomfoolery and I'll send you a FREE book as a thank you gift for subscribing:

Beth Bennet and Will Darcy help Anne de Bourgh find her happily ever after in

DANCING WITH THE COWBOY

My controlling grandma is planning my wedding. I'm just planning another encounter with the hot cowboy I met at the arts gala.

Gorgeous: Check
Flirty: Check
Looks good in rawhide trousers: Double check
He's a smart sharpshooter and my heart doesn't stand a chance.
SUBSCRIBE TO GIGI'S NEWSLETTER AND GET A FREE BOOK HERE

Prefer to binge read? Get the Vol 1 Box Set
Backstage Romance box set.

A NOTE FROM GIGI

Thanks a ton to my critique partners Rachael and Dawn. You are the best. I owe you so much.

And for Rachael Bastian, who was responsible for naming Reeses. I think it suits him well.

Also, a special shout out to my chat group on Instagram: the Sweet, Clean, Romance Authors Sorority. I love you to bits.

And finally, to my Early Blumers ARC group. You brighten my day with your encouragement and input. Readers like you are gold!

And for you, dear reader who found me in this vast sea of amazing books on Amazon. Thanks for taking a chance on me. I hope you enjoyed the book.

RECIPE

Biscochitos (anise seed cookies)
A Family Recipe
Makes 5 dozen

INGREDIENTS
- 1 lb shortening
- 1 ½ cups sugar
- 2 tsp anise (seed or extract)
- 2 eggs, beaten
- 6 cups flour
- 3 tsp baking powder
- 1 tsp salt
- ½ cup brandy or bourbon
- ¼ cup sugar
- 1 Tbl cinnamon

INSTRUCTIONS

Cream shortening, 1 ½ c sugar, and anise in a mixing bowl. Add eggs and beat well.

Combine flour, baking powder, and salt in a separate mixing bowl.

Alternating, add flour and brandy to creamed mix until a stiff dough is made.

Knead dough slightly and pat or roll to a ¼ or ½ inch thickness.

Cut dough into desired shapes.

Bake at 350 °F for 10 to 12 minutes.

Combine remaining sugar and cinnamon in a small mixing bowl. Dust the top of each cookie with a small amount

ABOUT THE AUTHOR

Gigi is a hopeless musical theatre nerd and sucker for happily-ever-afters.

Former professional wedding singer turned word-slinger, Gigi lives in Southern California with her personal chef...er...husband and two weird and awesome teenagers.

When Gigi's not writing like a crazy woman or hanging out with other authors on Instagram, she likes to binge-watch Doctor Who and spend all her free cash on Broadway shows and books.

Visit Gigi Blume's Website:
www.gigiblume.com

Instagram: @gigiblume
Facebook: @gigiblume
Pinterest: @gigiblumebooks
Twitter @gigi_blume

BOOKS BY GIGI BLUME

Backstage Romance Series

Confessions of a Hollywood Matchmaker

Love and Loathing

Dancing with the Cowboy

Secrets of a Hollywood Matchmaker

Driving Miss Darcy

The Friend Act

Made in the USA
Middletown, DE
22 June 2021